WYOMING WILDFLOWERS:
THE BEGINNING

Wyoming Wildflowers series
Prequel

Patricia McLinn

Dear Readers: If you encounter typos or errors in this book, please send them to me at Patricia@patriciamclinn.com. Even with many layers of editing, mistakes can slip through, alas. But, together, we can eradicate the nasty nuisances. Thank you! — Patricia McLinn

Join Patricia McLinn's Readers List and get news on releases and special deals first.
https://www.patriciamclinn.com/readers-list

Wyoming Wildflowers series
Wyoming Wildflowers: The Beginning (prequel)
Almost a Bride
Match Made in Wyoming
My Heart Remembers
Wyoming Wildflowers Trilogy (Books 2–4)
A New World (prequel to Jack's Heart)
Jack's Heart
Rodeo Nights (prequel to Where Love Lives)
Where Love Lives
A Cowboy Wedding
Wyoming Wildflowers Collection (Books 1–6, plus prequels)

Also available in audio

CHAPTER ONE

Denver—Thirty-five years ago

Wednesday

"C'mon, c'mon, hurry up! Nobody cares our bus broke down. Just want a good time at curtains up!"

"I swear, if he says the show must go on, I'll clobber him."

Donna Roberts laughed at her roommate's grumble. Lydia let the company's chief nagger get under her skin at the best of times. For Lydia, like most in their national touring production of "Sweet Charity," those best times came only when performing.

Now Lydia groaned. It also got under her skin that Donna was not among that *most*. "Don't tell me you can still laugh."

The two-and-a-half days since closing in Omaha *had* been tough. They'd also been a breath of fresh air and real life to Donna.

Not that being in a national touring company wasn't rewarding. The weeks of rehearsals in New York had been amazing. Learning songs and choreography had left her walking on air—metaphorically. Literally, her feet had ached like crazy. So, months on the road wore off the gloss. That was only natural.

"C'mon, c'mon," Brad shouted again. "Get your stuff to your rooms, get what you need, and back here in twenty."

"We would if we could," Lydia muttered.

Crew that had been on the bus should have been at the theater hours ago to prep for curtain. They'd slung bags into the lobby pell-mell sending arriving's routine confusion into chaos.

Donna slid off her coat to drape it on the lobby's old-fashioned banister. No way was she risking her prize to the protruding corners and edges of the luggage pile. She stepped over a bag, slid her foot into a crack, and stretched toward a slice of blue that might be…

"Sound-check top of the hour, everybody but Charity—"

"Sure, Miss TV Star gets a pass," Lydia hissed to Donna.

"—then run-through only before curtain. Run-through only!" Brad shouted. "Twenty! Not a second more. Go, go, *Go!*"

Donna shifted her weight to her front leg. She elbowed aside a knobby canvas bag with something protruding, and … Yes, it was her bag. If she could budge that duffel, which had to outweigh her, and the suitcase on top of it—

She stopped, frozen by the sensation of a spotlight trained on her, when she was neither on stage nor a star. Still, from her high school and college days, she wasn't unfamiliar with the experience. This brought similar warmth across her chest and throat, while her fingers and toes went cold, butterflies rioted in her stomach, and her heart swelled with a *rightness.* Yet this was different…

Yes, that was it. Each element was even warmer, even colder, even flightier, and carried far, far more rightness.

Slowly, she lifted her head.

A tall young man with broad shoulders stood at the edge of the company's chaos. He wore a blue-striped shirt tucked into jeans, topped by a plain tan winter jacket, and a dark brown cowboy hat. She had never seen a cowboy hat look more at home on anyone, including John Wayne and Steve McQueen.

He wasn't the most gorgeous man she'd ever seen. She'd been in the business for a year and a half now, and she'd seen a fair number of drop-dead gorgeous guys. Feature for feature, he didn't match up. No way.

Attractive, absolutely. Appealing, oh, yes. And something else … Real. That was it. *Real.*

He looked back at her steadily, almost solemnly.

Deep in his eyes, a light burned that she couldn't quite catch. Almost as if she glimpsed—Donna sucked in a breath.

The sound snapped her trance, and she broke the look.

What had gotten into her? He probably wasn't even looking at her. Most likely, she'd caught the edge of somebody else's spot. Plenty of the girls were knockouts—they sure were taller, with legs that went on and on and on, while Donna's just went.

He was probably looking at Lydia or Raeanne or MaryBeth or Nora. She hoped not Nora.

She looked back at the young man.

He was looking at her.

Only at her.

Her heart *ba-BOOM*ed like the bass drum.

"Let's go, let's go! C'mon, Roberts. You asleep in there?"

Donna jolted, nearly losing her balance. "My bag. Bottom—"

Before her mumble was half out, the tall young man strode forward, removed duffel and suitcase with ease, and scooped up her bag, presenting it to her like it weighed nothing.

She stared into steady gray eyes with a spark that—

"Roberts!" Brad shouted.

She grabbed the handles of her bag, and lugged it behind her as she retraced her path through the dwindling mass of bags. At the edge, she turned back. The young man stood where she'd left him, watching her.

"Thank you."

"Welcome." He smiled. And drop-dead gorgeous didn't hold a candle to him.

"Donna! Not holding this elevator if you don't get in now," Lydia yelled.

"Thank you very much!" She wheeled, grabbed her coat, and ran for the elevator.

Ed Currick remained where he was, watching the closed elevator door until physiology forced him to blink.

In his life he'd been thrown by horses, bulls, and a tractor. Nothing had ever knocked the breath out of him the way she had.

Entering from the street, he'd discovered the dignified, even stuffy atmosphere of the Rockton Hotel he'd left this morning transformed to a loud, energized, and disorganized scene.

He'd looked across the lobby at the crowd causing the hubbub, and there she'd been. Laughing.

The faces around her had been varying shades of intent, harried, cranky, drawn.

She was laughing.

She was the shortest in a cluster of young women, yet she'd held every bit of his attention. Then she'd taken off her coat, revealing curves perfectly proportioned to her height, and waded into the mountain of luggage like the adventure of a lifetime.

To that point he'd been intrigued.

Then she looked up and their gazes met…

It was like all the horses, bulls, and tractors he'd ever been on had gotten together and thrown him at once. Like he was lying flat, with not an atom of air left in his lungs, while something stronger and hotter expanded his heart until he was sure his chest wouldn't hold it, and all the while he stared into the dazzling sun.

"Are you okay, young man?"

He jerked his head around, only then realizing he'd stayed in place staring at the closed elevator door for who knew how long.

A tiny woman, easily as old as his grandmother, stood nearby, wrapped up in obvious preparation for going outside.

"Ma'am." He tipped his hat. "I'm fine, Ma'am."

"You look like you saw a ghost."

"No, Ma'am." And what he thought he saw he wasn't about to tell a soul. Ever.

Her gaze flicked to the elevator door, then back to him. "Hmph" was all she said before exiting.

He pulled in a breath, and damned if his chest didn't feel sore, almost like he *had* been thrown by a horse or a bull or a tractor.

Not that a little soreness mattered.

After every one of the throws he'd ever experienced, he'd not only gotten up off the ground, he'd eventually mastered the beast or machinery he'd been tackling. Most times after a lot of hard work and a few more rib-jolting throws, but he got there in the end.

He'd just do the same with *her*.

He felt his lips twist up. Well, not exactly the same. This was going to require a skill set that didn't enter into his daily life much. Nope, horse-sense, cow-sense, and mechanical aptitude weren't going to get him very far with her.

Her.

He hadn't even gotten her name. And that could be a real draw-back, since he intended to marry her.

CHAPTER TWO

Thursday

"Hey, you. You got one," Grover rumbled as he neared her.

The stage door keeper's announcement stopped Donna as she pulled on her coat, ready to leave for the night. He was looking right at her, so she must be "you." But his words didn't make sense.

Maybe double performances today on top of last night's scramble had caught up with her. Her legs were holding up okay, but apparently her mind had turned to jelly. "One?"

"Yep, and this one knows respect. Held the door for Maudie like a gentleman."

"One what?" she specified.

"Them stage-door-Johnnies. That's what I call 'em. When I'm being polite-like," Grover said.

She'd wondered yesterday when they'd returned to the lobby on the way to the theater ... but no one had been there. No one interesting.

"What're you looking at?" Lydia had demanded.

Donna had covered her three-sixty survey of the lobby with "Searching for signs of holiday cheer. Decorations are up lots of places."

Lydia had snorted. "What difference do holidays make to us? Just another day at the office."

Last night when they'd left the theater, Donna had squelched an urge to look around. That would have been silly. She wasn't the siren type.

"You must have me confused with one of the other girls." She gave Grover's arm a no-hard-feelings pat. "I'm Donna Roberts."

"No mistake. Donna Roberts. That's the one he wants." Grover wheezed with silent laughter at his double entendre.

Donna felt heat in her cheeks. Blushing. How stupid for a grown woman who was making a life in the theater for heaven's sakes. She wasn't some innocent from the Midwest. Not entirely.

But neither was she in the market for a tour-stop fling, as some in the company enjoyed, then forgot as soon as the bus pulled out. "As long as you both know you're ships passing in the night, it's fun," Lydia often said. "As long as you don't fall for one of them. Big mistake."

In theory, Donna saw the appeal. In practice, she'd never felt the inclination to try.

"I'm not interested," she told Grover now.

"Aw, see the boy," came Maudie's voice from behind her in the narrow corridor. Donna had never heard the woman's title with the company, probably because no title covered all the varied chores she did. "Couldn't have been kinder when he helped me at the door. Most don't see an old lady like me. He's a nice one."

"But Grover said—Well, you heard him."

"I heard. Just proves he's a male. What would you be wanting with one who didn't want that eventually? A lot of good he'd do you. But this one won't be after you for it before you say hello like some. Go meet the boy."

"No. I'm not interested. We're only here a short time." Even as she said the last sentence she realized its weakness. What did it matter how long they were in Denver if she wasn't interested?

"No reason to be afraid," Maudie said.

"I'm not afraid—"

"Go to the place around the corner. There'll be plenty of us in there to call out to if you're not comfortable."

Oh. That kind of afraid.

"Just don't be going back to the hotel alone. This Colfax Avenue isn't the worst area we've been in, but it's not the best, either. Fine with a crowd—or a young man who knows how to handle himself as he appears to be. Why they stick us way out here instead of with the rest of the theaters, I don't know."

"Hey," Grover objected. "Colfax got more soul than any Broadway or some such place. And Bonfils is a fine theater, so——"

"Oh, don't start with me about fine theaters. You might have done television in your day, but I've been in more theaters than you can begin to imagine, young man." Maudie drew herself up, taking advantage of Grover's open-mouthed blinking at being called a young man. "And don't change the subject from Donna meeting this boy. Now, if you'll move aside, she can get on her way."

"Go on," encouraged Grover, stepping back and wisely not engaging Maudie in further battle. "I don't want to be seeing that long face of his another night anyway."

"Another night?" Donna didn't budge.

Maudie peered at her. "That's right, second night he's been here. Meet the boy."

"Yeah," chorused Grover, "put him out of his misery and——"

"Fine." Donna wrapped her coat tight, holding the crossed-over material with her arm. She needed to sew buttons on her fabulous find, and she would, as soon as she found ones that matched those on the cuffs. "Only so you two will stop going on about it."

She moved past them, muttering about poor boy and pushy people as she swung open the stage door with emphasis.

The heavy door took some doing to get started, something she'd learned yesterday, since Grover rarely actually opened it. But in this moment, the resistance was gone, because someone was opening it from outside with far more *oomph* than she'd supplied.

The swing of the door carried her with it, causing her to step back, as Angela Ford, "Sweet Charity" and star of their company, glided in, drawing with her a billow of cold, snow-smelling air.

"Why thank you so much, honey," Angela said with the husky voice that added to her portrayal of Charity. She smiled up at the young man who had opened the door for her from outside.

Donna wouldn't have been flattered by *honey*, even if it had been meant for her. Angela called everyone *honey*, not bothering to pretend she knew their names. *Honey* made it onstage, too, when she forgot character names.

"I'll just get my umbrella. When I come back…"

"Thank you, ma'am, but—"

Donna saw the door-opener's mouth below the brim of his low-ered cowboy hat for a slice of a second—her heartbeat jumped tempo—before he raised his head. His eyes came to her. Her heart gave a lurching thud that threatened to buckle her knees.

Him.

The man from the hotel lobby.

"—I'm here to see Miss Roberts."

He held out a large, work-toughened, immaculately clean hand.

Donna was aware Angela's would-be chuckle held an edge—she wouldn't have appreciated that *ma'am*. And she *really* wouldn't have appreciated anyone, much less an attractive male, devoting attention to Donna instead of her.

"How sweet," Angela said, sweeping away. "Maudie! Maudie, I need you!"

Donna hardly noticed. With the man from the hotel lobby looking down at her with that same unsettling light in his eyes as yesterday, she concentrated on putting her hand in his with an appearance of calm. His hand closed around hers with a gentleness that indicated he did not abuse his strength.

Her heart did that lurching thud again, and his hand tightened as if he'd felt the same knee-buckling stumble.

"May I take you to supper, Miss Roberts?" A smile lightened the formality.

"At the diner around the corner," Maudie said from behind Don-na.

Angela also would not like Maudie ignoring her summons.

"Yes, ma'am," he said.

Donna felt a giggle rising at Angela's reaction if she knew he'd put her and Maudie in the same *ma'am* category.

"What's your name, young man?" Maudie demanded.

"Ed Currick, of the Slash-C Ranch in Knighton, Wyoming, ma'am." He used his free hand to tip his hat to Maudie.

"Well, see that you behave yourself, Ed Currick of the Slash-C Ranch in Knighton, Wyoming." Maudie's sternness was counteracted by her giving Donna a firm shove on the back to send her toward him, then closing the stage door behind her.

They stood in the stark brightness of the security light. He—Ed Currick—was so much taller that she had to tip her head back to look into his face, and that did no good because the light beating down on his cowboy hat left his face in shadow.

"Are you a cowboy?"

"You might say so. I'm a rancher, Donna."

Something about the way he said her name made her abruptly aware that he still held her hand. She drew free, overlapped the edges of her coat more tightly.

"Right. You mentioned a ranch. If you haven't eaten you don't want to go to the diner. It's mostly sandwiches."

"Your friend will worry if we're not there."

She smiled. "Maudie's a company institution, but she doesn't have to decide where we eat."

"Your friend will worry if we're not there," he repeated. Apparently that settled it for him.

And she supposed he was right. Maudie would worry. "A sandwich is good for me, but I suspect it takes more to fill you up."

"It'll do fine." He stepped back, raising a palm-up hand inviting her to walk past him, then turned in beside her.

They walked in silence to where this alley alongside the building intersected the sidewalk fronting the theater. She was aware of him slowing his pace to accommodate her. Some men didn't bother. Some men made a production of it. He simply gentled his pace to match her shorter stride.

"Grover and Maudie said you were here last night."

"I was."

"You saw the show?"

"Yep."

"Both nights?" She turned the corner onto the sidewalk and nearly came to a standstill as a gust of wind hit her in the face.

"Yep."

She looked up at an angle, squinting against the wind. "You didn't come backstage last night?"

"I did."

"But…" Her first thought was of her temptation to look around when they left last night. He had been there. Did that mean—No. It didn't mean anything.

"You came out with two other girls," he said, "all talking about how tired you were, how you were going right back to the hotel for hot baths, and a good night's sleep before today's two shows."

"Oh."

One side of his mouth quirked up. "A smart man knows better than to try to compete with that."

The wind had eased, letting her look at him without her eyes watering. "Are you a smart man, Ed Currick?"

"Passable smart."

She laughed at the assumed deadpan humility.

They reached the diner. He moved ahead to open the door.

"Two nights in a row? You must like musical theater."

"Can't say. Didn't pay much attention to most of it. I came to see you."

She was saved from needing to respond by the business of entering the small restaurant, finding a table, and taking her chair. A tableful of company members waved, eyebrows waggling suggestively at her companion's back.

She ignored them, arranging her coat over her chair. He'd offered to hang it up, but she liked to keep it close. She didn't expect anyone to take it, but she'd be so heartbroken if they did that it didn't seem worth the risk. Then she concentrated on the menu. It didn't require much time.

Finally, Donna gave Ed Currick of Knighton, Wyoming a stiff smile. What was she doing here with him? Not only were they a pair of Lydia's ships passing in the night, while she was more of a permanent mooring type—if that meant what she thought it meant—but what did they have in common? What would they talk about?

He looked back. Those steady gray eyes had a darker rim around the edge, and lashes that were long and full, yet took nothing away from the overt masculinity of a strong-featured face.

He'd removed his cowboy hat, and there was a hat-shaped dent in his thick dark hair. Her fingers itched to delve into it—only to fix the dent, of course.

Heat flowed through her.

Oh, Lord, her hormones were *not* thinking about talking.

"So are you or aren't you a cowboy?" It came out abrupt. Strange. She was usually so good with people.

He's a man, *not people*, some voice inside her head said.

Definitely, certainly a man.

"Ranching calls for some cowboying."

"What else does it call for?"

"A fair amount of everything." People who weren't paying attention, weren't looking into his eyes might miss the glint of humor.

"That doesn't tell me—"

The solitary waitress, harried by the influx of theater people, rushed up. He ordered two beef sandwiches, a salad, fries, and a milkshake to her sandwich and cup of soup.

"Is it always like that?" he asked with the waitress gone.

"Like what?"

He tipped his head backward toward the boisterous table behind him.

"Pretty much. Sort of like when a family with lots of siblings gets together." She was careful not to make eye-contact with any of the table's occupants. Especially Lydia or Henri.

"And yesterday afternoon? At the hotel?"

"Not usually that bad." She laughed. Then made a discovery that stopped her breath in her throat and started her heart hammering like she'd danced back-to-back-to-back numbers.

Steady gray eyes could burn.

She thought it had been a fluke in the lobby. It wasn't. The spotlight of his eyes concentrated heat inside her like she'd never known. Those eyes could burn ... and they could ignite.

She sucked in air, but it brought with it the heat from his eyes. So now it was inside as well as surrounding her. She'd go right up in flames completely, if she didn't ... didn't...

"They're letting off steam. We've had a hectic week," she said in rush. "We closed in Omaha Sunday night. Traveling on Monday is normal, but instead of having Tuesday off, we were supposed to rehearse for last night's benefit and today's two. A tough schedule even if everything went right."

"But something went wrong."

"Exactly. First, road construction. Brad fussed at him, so the driver tried a detour of the detour. *Then* our bus broke down. Usually our truck travels with, but because of the tight schedule it left Sunday night with whatever crew squeezed in to start on set-up. So, we were alone. It was mid-afternoon before help came. We were all wearing pounds of clothing by then. The mechanic says he can't repair the bus in time to get us here. They send for another bus, but in the meantime there we all are—well, not the crew that went ahead, or the principals or conductor, because they're driven separately, but the ensemble, and orchestra, and some of the crew, and—anyway, we're crammed into this tiny, isolated service station, devouring every crumb from the vending machines, because we hadn't had lunch or dinner. Then something amazing happens."

He still watched her intently, but the flame in his eyes had lowered. A smolder now. Not nearly as unsettling—no, not unsettling. She wasn't unsettled. Just cautious.

"What was amazing?"

She blinked, abruptly realizing she'd been staring into his eyes. And he'd been staring back.

"People." She swallowed, cleared her throat and started again. "People started showing up, a whole stream of pickups. They loaded us all up, and took us to a church. By now it was dark and cold and we were *so* hungry, but this church glowed with lights from every window, and when we stepped inside—" She closed her eyes, breathing in remembered aromas and sounds. "—it was like coming home on Thanksgiving, having all those wonderful scents and the swell of welcoming voices. Oh, how I missed that."

It had been tough last week. Missing her favorite meal, missing her family even more, missing being where she was loved. But that was to be expected. Part of being a professional. Paying those dues.

"You weren't home for Thanksgiving?"

"Not this year. I got home for Thanksgiving and Christmas last year. I could make my own schedule because I wasn't steadily employed," she said dryly.

"What did you do when you weren't steadily employed?"

"Kept trying to *be* steadily employed. I had a few small things, then a nice off-off Broadway show last winter. Short run, unfortunately. Otherwise, it's casting calls and classes and waitressing so I don't have to beg from my parents—not that they wouldn't help. They've always encouraged us to go for our dreams. It's just that they worry. You know, New York, the theater."

"Here." The waitress plopped a plate with two big sandwiches in front of her. Ed efficiently swapped the plates.

"So folks had gathered at the church because word got around about a busload of people needing help," he prompted.

"How did you know?"

He shrugged.

"Well, you're right. People brought blankets, cots, sleeping bags so we'd be comfortable sleeping in the church. But first—"

"First you ate." Lines fanned from his eyes like ripples of smiles.

"Now, how'd you know *that?*"

"It's the way people are in this part of the world."

"Oh." So his—Knighton?—was like the people at that church? She didn't think it could get any more different from New York City. Though, perhaps, not so very different from Indiana. "Well, you're right. We ate. *Such* good food. Even the ones who fuss about weight piled up their plates. And cookies? Delicious. They had Christmas cookies already—What's your favorite Christmas cookie?"

"Chocolate chip."

She *ts*ked. "Those are for everyday. You have to have special cookies at Christmas."

"Christmas is a day, too. Chocolate chip," he insisted.

"Fine. So, in *addition* to chocolate chip, what kind of cookies?"

"These chocolate bar things with a little crust under them and nuts on top."

"Those sound good. What are they called?"

"The chocolate bar things with a little crust—Ow." Like her light swat on his arm made an impression ... although she *had* felt a tingle. "Okay, Mom calls them toffee bars. What's your favorite?"

"Cutout cookies. And butter cookies we make into tree shapes or wreaths with a cookie press, then decorate."

"I'd probably eat a few of those," he said judiciously.

"You'd have eaten more than a few of the ones at that church. We repaid them the only way they'd let us, by literally singing for our supper."

He smiled, and she had an instant, vivid flash of two images blending together. Like seeing a double exposure, this one held an image of a toddler and another one of an older man with gray streaking his hair. Yet both had the exact same grin, like they were related. And ... Yes, a *third* exposure, another image, this one of the man in front of her. And it was his grin she saw. His grin shared with the toddler and the older man. She wanted to wrap her arms around all of them, because seeing them made her heart—

"You okay, Donna?" His low voice reached her from far away, then an electric current connected with her hand. She jolted. "Sorry.

Didn't mean to startle you."

She looked from where his hand covered hers on the table, to his no-longer-smiling face. Definitely the face she'd seen. As it was now, but also the toddler's and the older man's. How strange. How very strange.

"Donna?"

"I'm fine. Really. I…" She slid her hand from under his, picked up her sandwich. "What was I saying?"

"Singing for your supper."

"Right," she nodded. "We started with numbers from the show— the parts suitable for a church. I did Charity, since I'm the understudy. And they applauded and cheered, and some sang along. It was like when I fell in love with dancing and singing."

"And acting?"

"That came later, to wrap it all together. Dad says I came out of the womb dancing and singing. Mom worked like crazy with the lessons and rehearsals and recitals." Impulsively, she put her hand on his arm. "Do you have something you feel passionately about?"

"The Slash-C. That C's for Currick. Been in the family for genera-tions. It's … home."

She caught her breath at the way he said the last word.

He might have felt it, too, because he turned the subject. "So you sang from your show for the people at the church."

"Then we all sang Christmas carols as we cleaned up. We stood in the doorway, singing 'Silent Night' as they drove off, and it started to snow. It was … magical. The best experience since—"

Abruptly she became aware they were holding hands across the table. She drew her hand free to fold her napkin, telling how the replacement bus didn't arrive until late Tuesday.

They drove through the night and into Wednesday, the hours tick-ing down toward that night's show. The scramble, with so little time and a new theater and everyone tired. And then two shows today. "Wildest days of the whole tour," she concluded.

He asked more about her time in New York, and she answered

readily. When he asked where else the tour had been, she rattled off what felt like a Greyhound bus schedule, ending with "…then Omaha, then here. My first time to see the Rocky Mountains, even if it is from a distance."

"New theater every week?"

"Sometimes. Sometimes less, sometimes more. So, tell me about your ranch," she said. Not the smoothest transition, but a crease had appeared between his strong brows, and she wanted to change the subject to see if it would go away.

"Ranch is in the same place every day," he said. She thought that was more of his deadpan humor but wasn't sure since he was looking around, not meeting her eyes.

The final group of her fellow company members got up to leave, talking and yawning and waving.

"Ma'am? May we have our check, please?" Ed asked the waitress. Then he addressed Donna, "You ready?"

She looked at her plate, barely remembering what she'd eaten, and yet with a sudden, odd emptiness. "I guess I am."

"We'll follow along with your friends, so you're not feeling like you're walking alone so late with a stranger," he said as he paid.

The emptiness in her disappeared. He wasn't hurrying their departure for any reason other than consideration.

He stood, holding her coat.

It was a courtesy she appreciated. Not because she wasn't a capable and independent woman, but because getting into a coat could be awkward, what with heavy layers to contend with. Women should help men with their coats, too.

She slid one arm in, holding the cuff of her sweater with her fingers so it didn't bunch up.

That was when she felt the warm wall of his chest behind her. Not touching, but so *there*. He still held her coat while she twisted to insert her second cuff-holding hand into the opposite sleeve, so his arms resembled a ballerina's in first position with her in the center. Only anything less like a ballerina's delicacy was hard to imagine. He was solid heat, surrounding her, tempting her.

She missed the armhole.

"Sorry," he murmured, his breath stirring her hair, adding a shiver to the heat transferring from his body deep into hers.

"My fault." She bit her lip, concentrating on getting her hand in. She flurried into words. "I love this coat, but it does have narrow sleeves. The price you pay for high fashion."

Success. Her arm was in the sleeve.

"Is it warm?"

With both arms coated, she continued her motion to pivot, feeling somehow that facing him would remove this sense of sinking into his heat.

Except he didn't release her coat, so he still was connected to her and the spotlight sensation returned in full force. As bright, hot and direct as before.

Warm? Oh, yes, very warm.

She sucked in a breath, then let it out on a stream of words.

"Warm doesn't matter. I had fantastic luck finding this coat at a thrift store in New York—designer, with hardly any wear, and I got it for a steal. Of course, it needs a belt for the full 007 trench coat effect."

"It's red," he said, a hand at the small of her back. "Bright red."

"I especially love that. It lifts my spirits no matter what."

He reached past her to open the door. "Can't imagine a spy wearing a red coat."

She laughed. "Maybe not an ordinary spy. But James Bond doesn't blend in, so why should I?"

"You wouldn't ever blend in."

The depth of his voice had a strange effect, threatening her ability to stay upright. A wind from nowhere buffeted her and swung one side of her coat wide, plastering it against his legs.

"You'll freeze out here. You should button up."

"Can't. No buttons."

He frowned. "Designers make coats with no buttons?"

"Sure, some do. But in this case, someone apparently cut them off. So, until I find the buttons, I do this—" She overlapped the front edges and wrapped her arms around herself.

"You need a warm coat. You're in Denver, not Atlanta." That was one of the stops she'd mentioned. Of course they'd been *there* during a heat wave.

"Only for—" She didn't know exactly. "—a few days."

"Days? You can freeze to death in hours."

"I'm not going to freeze to death. Look at how nice it is now." The errant gust was gone, the night still and crisp. There were enough people on the streets to not feel isolated. Holiday decorations enlivened windows of stores and businesses.

"It can turn not-nice real fast. It's nearly December, and—" He gestured to the poster of a familiar red-clad figure in a nearby window. "—there's a reason Santa wears fur."

She chuckled. "He doesn't care about style, and I do. So, what brings you to Denver?"

He raised his eyebrows. "You know, even a cowpuncher recognizes a change of subject."

"I'm glad he does, though I have no idea why someone would punch a cow."

"To get the cow to move. Though *cowpoke*'s more accurate. Can't say I've ever seen anyone punch a cow, even if Alex Karras supposedly did it to a horse in 'Blazing Saddles.' "

"You've seen that movie?"

"Yes'm. Them there talkin' picture shows came to Wyoming a *leetle* while back now."

"I didn't—" She started to apologize if he thought she'd implied his state was backward. Then she spotted mischief in his eyes. "Okay, I deserved that. Now, back to what brings you to Denver."

"That wasn't to change the subject from your not having a warm coat?"

"At first," she admitted, and he chuckled, "but now I want to know. What brought you here?"

"Stock."

"*Really?* But it's winter."

He smiled. "Not your kind of stock. My kind—livestock."

She laughed. And found him looking at her with warmth, approval, appreciation, and something more. He struck her as someone more inclined to smile than laugh, yet he enjoyed her laughing as much as she enjoyed it herself.

"How egocentric, thinking stock meant summer stock theater and how snobby, being surprised there'd be any here. Especially since I grew up in Indiana, not exactly a hot bed of theater."

"Well, what I'm here for *is* a stock show. But nothing like what you do."

"You know about summer stock theater?"

"I've seen a black and white movie or two on TV."

"Ah, Judy Garland and Mickey Rooney," she said wisely.

"My primary resource for information on the theater."

"Then you can't blame me for basing my ranch knowledge on 'Bonanza' and 'The Big Valley.' "

"Wrong century, but we don't take much to new-fangled ways, so you're fine." She giggled. He smiled. "So, you're from Indiana? Farm girl?"

She shook her head. "Not unless you count driving past them. But tell me about this stock show. Is it a big deal?"

"The big one's in January, but folks I wanted to talk to were coming to this, so I arranged to get away."

"December? January? I can think of better times to come to Denver—unless you're a skier."

He grinned. "Less of a skier than a roper."

"Around the ranch," she said with a nod. "Like 'Bonanza.' "

"That and rodeo."

"Rodeo? So you *are* a cowboy?"

He slanted her a look. "You got a special fondness for cowboys?"

There was meaning in the question, and there would be meaning in her answer. No matter what answer she gave.

She met his gaze, and said, "I don't know. Yet."

She was caught by a flare in his eyes. Still, his words and tone were mild. "Fair enough."

This undercurrent could tug her right out to sea … where their ships would be passing each other, heading opposite directions, just like Lydia always said.

"So, rodeo … You're one of those who gets thrown from a horse?"

"Not if I can help it." A grin accompanied his dry words. "Used to do some bronc riding—bare and saddle. A little steer wrestling. But as my mom says, there's not much difference between getting thrown from a bronc and throwing yourself off a perfectly good horse to wrestle a steer. Mostly I focus on roping events."

"Your mom," she repeated, ignoring broncs, getting thrown, or wrestling a steer. All of which sounded disturbingly dangerous.

Not that mothers weren't.

"Yeah. She's something else. Third-generation Wyoming. Grew up on a ranch. Knows more about horses and cattle than any other ten people. Dad always says he knew marrying her meant marrying a herd, too. She'd like you."

"How on earth can you know that?" A ranch woman like Mrs. Currick was far more likely to see a singer-dancer with Broadway aspirations as flighty, if not a downright floozy. Maybe she could win her over—

What? Wait. What was she doing, thinking of winning over this unknown woman?

"She'd like you because I do," Ed said.

She looked into the gray heat of his eyes and her mental protest evaporated to nothing. No, not to nothing. It converted to steam. Steam that filtered through her bloodstream and pooled in her lungs, consuming all her oxygen. Until she gasped to draw in more.

Just as she did, he leaned down and touched his mouth to hers.

It was a gentle kiss, undemanding. He seemed careful not to crowd her with his greater height and size.

A mouth against a mouth. That's all.

All … Yes, that's what it was. All. All of her. All of him. All of the universe.

He was the universe, surrounding her. His presence and the mingled scent of warm man and cold air rippled around her, while drawn-in breaths brought the tastes and scents of him inside her.

She wanted to step into him, to refuge against him.

She wanted to open her mouth, to taste the promised heat.

She wanted to touch him, to feel the faint lines at the corners of his eyes and mouth, the strength promised by those shoulders.

She wanted…

She wanted.

With a gasp that came as much from shock as oxygen deprivation, she stepped back.

"I've got to … I should…" She gestured over her shoulder to the hotel's entry. "Go inside."

"We're going the same way."

"Oh. Yes. Of course."

He held the door, then followed her in and to the elevator, where he pressed the up button. Her heartbeat went from the lightest high-hat flutter straight to bass drum. She stood beside him. Silent. Unable to say anything, think anything.

The elevator came, the door sliding open, the car yawning before her. Them. He urged her forward with his warm hand at the small of her back—warmth so vivid that even through coat, sweater, and shirt she could pinpoint each cell experiencing it.

Only when she was inside and turned to face the door did she realize he hadn't followed her.

"Good night, Donna."

"Good night, Ed."

The door slid closed. The lurch as the elevator rose explained her wobbly knees. But what explained the wide-eyed look of … *shock?* that stared back from the door's polished metal surface?

CHAPTER THREE

Thursday night

Three of the girls tumbled into the room she shared with Lydia, demanding to know all about "The Cowboy."

"Rancher," she said.

"Looked like you were having a good time," Lydia said. "Talking and laughing."

"Uh-huh." She answered absently, preoccupied by the realization of how easily they'd talked. On the walk back, the few silences had been relaxed and comfortable.

Except for the silence when they'd kissed. Definitely not relaxed.

"Talk about what a man should look like—yum," Raeanne said.

"Just those shoulders. Those are something a girl could sink her teeth into."

"Please, MaryBeth, don't tell us those details," Lydia begged.

"Totally wasted on Donna, of course," said Nora.

Ignoring the decidedly wasp-tongued Nora made life easier, so Donna didn't dispute the comment. But she'd had a couple serious relationships in college, had even discussed marriage with Jeff.

She'd shared a normal amount with her girlfriends about those relationships, and had been in on conversations with these girls about their admirers in various cities. She just didn't feel like sharing this evening with Ed.

Especially with Nora in her audience.

Lydia propped her hands on her hips and said to Nora, "Just because *you* raise the men-in-a-lifetime average doesn't mean everybody has to."

"He looked like he was a real gentleman," Raeanne said, jumping in to keep that animosity from flaring yet again.

Donna picked up by singing a phrase about being waited on by a guy like he was a maître d' from "If My Friends Could See Me Now," *Sweet Charity*'s best-known song, with Raeanne, MaryBeth, and Lydia joining in on the last phrase.

"Except your cowboy's even better because he's not looking to get tipped like a maître d'," Raeanne said.

"No, he's looking to get something else entirely." Nora smirked.

Lydia glared at her. "So what if he is, Donna has the right to a sex life. As long as she remembers they're ships passing in the night and not to get tangled up."

Nora rose from her spot on Donna's bed. She still moved fairly well, but the smoking and drinking were definitely showing. There were rumbles she might not have the role of Helene much longer. Some said because she'd be taking over the lead when Angela moved on and up. Some thought otherwise.

"As long as she doesn't get other ideas," Nora said. "Men aren't looking for a girl to take home to mother when they hang out at stage doors, not even when they see little Donna."

No one disputed that. Although Ed *had* said—No. That was just … conversation.

Lydia said staunchly, "Doesn't make any difference, since Donna's only looking for fun."

Then she looked at Donna, who couldn't do anything but agree. "Exactly. It's probably all moot, anyway. I doubt I'll ever see him again."

"God, *moot*," Nora mocked. "Another of your college girl words."

Nora never let it be forgotten that Donna had *wasted time* getting a college degree before pursuing a life in theater. Unlike—according to Nora—*real* theater people.

With the door now open and one of her extremely long legs curled around the edge of it the way she did in "Hey, Big Spender," Nora said, "I'll tell you what's not *moot*—what'll happen to you girls if Angela hears you singing any of Charity's songs, even in the shower. Not even little Donna's cowboy could save you."

On that exit line she was gone.

It broke the party up. "Because she's right," as MaryBeth said in a carefully low voice. "Nora might be a cat, but Angela's a tiger."

Donna didn't sleep much.

Perhaps because of the conversation. Perhaps from considering what might happen if two ships that passed in the night came across each other a second night. Or, perhaps, because of the time she spent staring at the ceiling, realizing Ed hadn't said a word about seeing each other again.

Did she feel it?

She'd never mentioned being involved. If she were, she would have said. She was too honest not to.

That didn't guarantee she felt anything for him.

She had to. This couldn't be all on his side.

Couldn't be.

Did she feel it?

He thought so. In the moment her sweet mouth touched his, he'd felt no doubt. That wonderful mouth, so generous in smiling and laughing … And kissing.

But lying here alone in bed, Ed couldn't be sure.

And it wasn't like they had time on their side.

Before those moments in the hotel lobby Wednesday afternoon, he'd been ready to return to the Slash-C. So eager to start putting into action ideas picked up here that he'd planned to move around Sunday appointments to be able to leave Saturday.

Not now.

God, all they had was Friday, Saturday, Sunday.

But he wouldn't rush her.

No matter what.

No matter how much he wanted her. No matter what he saw in her eyes. No matter how little time they had. He wouldn't do that to her.

She had to feel this, too.

CHAPTER FOUR

Friday

Relief so strong it smarted her eyes was Donna's first reaction.

Ed Currick stood outside the elevator when its door opened at the lobby the next morning. As if he'd stood sentry all night. Except he had shaved. And dampness in his hair and across the shoulders of his jacket showed he'd been outside in the flurries she'd noticed from her room window.

Still, the notion that he'd stood here, in the spot where she'd left him, pooled irrational warmth in the pit of her stomach.

She was going to see him again. She *was* seeing him again.

"Ed."

Relief, and maybe something else.

"Good morning, Donna. You said you like to see the towns you're in, and I hope you'll see some of Denver this morning with me, then have lunch."

She tried to keep her smile from stretching too wide. It was daylight, and their ships weren't passing. They were standing face to face—

"Excuse me. The rest of us would like to get off the elevator." Lydia's voice from behind her made Donna jump.

She and Ed moved sideways. "Oh, sorry! Uh—"

"Hi, I'm Lydia, Donna's roommate." She stuck out a hand, and he shook it as the others started past, blatantly studying Ed. "And you're Ed, and now I'll make my much desired exit."

"Nice meeting you, Lydia."

"You, too, Ed." She waved, then called to the others, "Wait up."

Perhaps in response to Lydia's call, MaryBeth turned back toward them, her words reaching them clearly: "…if he does, we'll get a week off from her dragging us to dusty old museums."

Lines fanned out from the corners of Ed's eyes, though his mouth remained straight. "So, if I take you to dusty old museums, I can win points with you *and* your friends."

As if he needed any added points with them. Or her.

"You'd think I was trying to kill them by getting them to know a little about the towns we're in," she said. "I don't even try to get them on tours anymore. You should have heard——"

"You do have a way of showing up at my door," came the familiar—if not quite as famous as its owner liked to think—voice of Angela Ford from behind Donna. By stepping aside from the first elevator, she and Ed had moved in front of another, this one a direct trip to the exclusive floors.

Angela addressed Ed, and only Ed. She placed a hand on his arm.

Donna supposed Angela meant it to look as if she were gently guiding him out of her way. More like the woman was holding on to him with no hint of letting go.

"Morning, Ma'am."

Ed reached up to touch the brim of his hat, easily dislodging Angela's hold, at the same time grasping Donna's elbow and drawing her to his side with his other hand.

"Good morning, Angela." She added a bright smile.

"Oh. Good morning." She looked from one to the other of them. Her smile disappeared. "My car's waiting."

With that, she swept past.

"Family, huh? Wasn't that what you said last night?" Ed said, as the exterior doors swung closed.

She chuckled. "Every family has a few difficult cases."

"So, what do you want to see first?"

"Oh, Ed, I'm sorry. I can't. I would love to, but I have to be at the theater. That's where we're all heading. Well, I don't know where Angela's going. But the rest of us. With everything going on, there hasn't been a run-through for understudies." It was her favorite part of their routine. But now, for the first time, she would have willingly given it up. "But after lunch—"

He shook his head. "I have afternoon meetings."

"Oh."

"Would you go to dinner with me? Supper I guess, after the show?"

"I can't. I have—" She stopped dead, a sudden idea speeding through her head.

"Plans," he filled in evenly. "I'm not surprised. I should have asked last night, but…"

His eyes dropped to her mouth. Her breath disappeared. He hadn't asked her about tonight's plans last night because he'd been busy kissing her. Busy kissing her and being kissed back by her.

"No, no. I was going to say—well, yes, I was going to say I have plans, but not those kinds of plans. It's just … it's the opening night party, and even though we have them in about every town, they want us to go, mingle with the community, important people."

"I understand. It's part of your job." He sounded relieved.

"Yes, it is. Only—"

"Like going to the stock show for me."

"Yes. Only—"

"We have responsibilities and—what?"

She had her hands on her hips and was looking up at him. Possibly glaring up at him. "For someone who started off not talking much, you're making it hard to get a word in edgewise."

He grinned. She thought it might not be good that he grinned when she was probably glaring at him. But that thought was way, way down in her reactions, compared to how that grin spread warmth across her skin and little jigs of pleasure under it.

"Sorry, Donna. Go ahead." And then there was the way he said her name…

"Okay. What I was going to say…" She seriously doubted her expression came close to a glare now. She shook herself. "Would you like to come to the opening night party?"

"With you?"

"Of course with me," she said indignantly. Did he think she was fixing him up with somebody? Angela, maybe? Hah!

His grin broadened. "Yes. I'd like that a lot."

"So, Angela heard you singing a Charity number, huh?" Nora asked as they filed into the shared dressing room after the last curtain call.

Shared, yet with placements in the dressing room as finely tuned as the billing. Nora, playing Helene, and Lydia, playing Nikki, had individual makeup tables and mirrors. The rest of them shared a communal set-up.

"No," Donna responded without much interest.

She'd had the oddest feeling on stage tonight. When she'd noticed it, she'd remembered a similar feeling last night. She didn't recall it from yesterday's matinee. Had it been there Wednesday night, too? She thought it might have been.

"Well, something was going on," Lydia said. "Even Angela doesn't usually miss her mark that many times."

"And wasn't it strange how when she did, it kept blocking out Donna?" Raeanne said earnestly. "What?"

Nora clicked her tongue impatiently. Lydia rolled her eyes.

Maudie stepped in. "That hem's about to come out again," she said to MaryBeth, who obediently took off her costume and handed it to a waiting wardrobe assistant. Maudie patted Raeanne on the shoulder. "They know Angela was blocking out Donna. That's why they're talking about her missing her marks."

"Oh."

"So, what did you do to our star?" Nora insisted.

Lydia's lips parted, then she met Donna's gaze through the double reflections—her mirror and Donna's—and closed her mouth.

MaryBeth was looking only at her own reflection as she began to remove her makeup. "I bet it has something to do with that guy. The Cowboy."

"Ya think?" Nora mocked.

Before she could say more, Angela swirled in, still in costume and makeup, as if fresh from additional solo curtain calls. When they all knew there hadn't been any after the last cast bow.

The room went still. Angela did not mingle with the rest of them. Ever.

"Ah, Maudie, there you are dear, I do need your assistance." She looked around the room, as if suddenly realizing where she was, then bestowed a smile on all.

Her entrance had carried her down the length of the shared makeup table. Now she stopped near where Donna sat.

She reached out absently, and picked up the silver-handled brush Donna's parents had given her. "How lovely," she murmured, then added immediately in full voice, "A lovely performance tonight, everyone. Lovely. Particularly you, hon."

She beamed at Donna, and started toward the door. "Maudie?" she invited—or ordered—the other woman to precede her, with a wave of Donna's brush.

"Thanks, Angela," Lydia said, snagging the brush out of her hand as she passed.

She gave a trill of a laugh. "How silly of me." Then was gone.

Nora got up and closed the door, then stood with her back to it. "Now do you believe me?"

"About what?" asked Raeanne, ever the straight-woman.

"That Angela is on the warpath against Donna," Nora said with relish. "And it's going to tear this company apart."

"Oh, for—"

Donna talked over Lydia. "I've never done anything to her, and I'm sure she would tell you the same thing."

"You don't have to have—"

The bang on the door made Nora yelp and the rest of them jump. "Half-hour! Half-hour to stage!"

"Good God, now Brad's timing us to get into our street clothes."

"It's only because of the party tonight," Raeanne explained kindly. "You know he likes us all to be on hand from the start to meet the important local people."

"I'm going to murder him," Lydia grumbled, but absently.

Because they had all buckled down to the serious business of getting ready.

Donna found Ed waiting for her by the stage door, in close conversation with Grover. She wondered about that, but had more immediate concerns.

Those stemmed from Lydia's incredulous response just now when Donna had said she'd invited Ed to the party.

"You did *what?* Are you crazy?"

"I don't see what harm it can do—"

"Oh, let's see. Number one, Angela. Think barracuda. And you're about to toss lunch in the pool. Number two, he's a *cowboy*."

"Rancher," Donna had murmured.

Lydia either didn't hear or ignored the correction. "You did see the end of 'Blazing Saddles,' didn't you? Where the cowboy types crash through the studio walls and get into a brawl with the musical types?"

"That was just silliness."

"All good humor is based on truth," Lydia declared haughtily. "The two do not mix. What is your cowboy going to think when some of the boys hit on him? Number three," she pursued, "ships passing in the night do not get entangled. Are you getting entangled?"

"No, of course not."

She might have undercut her denial by speeding away to find Ed and escort him to the party.

At the entrance to the stage, which had been transformed for the occasion into a buffet with open bar, she held him back with a hand on his arm.

"Uh, Ed, you know, uh, theater people are probably different from a lot you've met."

"You're different from anyone I've met."

Heat spread, inside and out, making it difficult to catch her breath. "I don't mean me, I mean … uh, some of the guys are not like you." Now, why had she addressed that, when what she really wanted to do was warn him about Angela.

His face went solemn, but she saw the telltale glint in his eyes. "You know, I haven't spent much time in big cities, but you'd be amazed the things we see on the ranch. Did you know some bulls prefer other bulls to cows?"

Three sounds came simultaneously: Her gasp of *"Really?"*, Ed's chuckle, and the urgent call of her name.

"Donna!" An executive with the company producing the tour rushed up. His job was to grab spots on theaters' future schedules. "Didn't you go to school out in the middle of the country?"

"There are lots of schools in the middle of the country. Which one? I went to Indiana University, but—No, wait—"

"That's the one—" Randall Witmeyer was already tugging her across the stage. "A member of the board went there and saw it in your Playbill bio. Need you to charm and delight as you always do."

"But—Ed?"

"Don't worry." Ed smiled. "I'll be fine."

She saw he *was* fine, even as she was thrust at the elderly member of the board like a sacrifice in front of a cranky god. Lydia hooked an arm in Ed's, and Donna felt a little better. A little later, Maudie joined them, and then she relaxed enough to truly concentrate on the board member.

They had a good time talking about the Bloomington campus, and how it had changed from his years there to hers. Such a good time that when they parted, with his wife insisting he meet the orchestra's director, Donna had lost track of Ed.

A jolt hit her bloodstream as she spotted him.

A second jolt hit when she realized neither Maudie nor Lydia was with him, but Angela was.

Before she took a step toward him, a voice behind her left ear said, "Who knew you could find anyone that presentable from Denver?"

Henri played Vittorio Vidal as well as forming part of the ensemble. He and Donna had hit it off immediately. Possibly because she listened to the ups and downs of his stormy relationship with Brad with care combined with drama-dampening matter-of-factness.

Over her shoulder, he also looked across the room at Ed, who was talking with the chair of the theater's board of directors, the top executive, Randall Witmeyer, and Angela.

"Not Denver," she said absently. "Knighton, Wyoming. Actually, a ranch outside it."

"Oh, my. You mean the cowboy hat's the real thing?"

"The real thing."

He moved around to beside her, peering into her face. "Oh, my," he repeated, with entirely different inflection.

"What?"

"Nothing." He turned back toward Ed and the others. "He seems to be holding his own with the locals *and* our tribe. Impressive."

"I know," she said.

"No visible signs of our Angel of Death feasting on him."

She forced herself to not chew her lip. "You don't think so?"

"Not a one. He's obviously talented in sidestepping and pretending deafness. He was telling me earlier—"

She twisted around, grabbed Henri by the shirt, and placed him so she could see him and Ed at the same time. "You were talking to him? What did you say? What did you tell him?"

"Not a thing! I swear." He dropped his innocent hands and act. "Except what a wonder our Donna is."

"Henri, you didn't … You weren't too outrageous were you?"

"Outrageous? *Moi?*"

At that moment, Ed looked over and gave her a small part of his smile, a public version of ones he'd given her alone, and even that pale edition was enough to have Henri returning to his, "Oh, my," and fanning himself. He sighed. "What a shame that isn't a 'Midnight Cowboy' kind of hat."

Donna laughed and swatted him. "You're as bad as he is."

"Oh, that sounds delightful. Do tell."

But she'd headed toward Ed, and she wasn't going to postpone to explain to Henri. Especially not since Ed's smile widened with each step she took.

They were strangers with a mutual attraction. Okay, a strong mutual attraction. A *very* strong mutual attraction.

Last night's kiss…

No. They were strangers. More important, she'd never entered a relationship she didn't think might have a future, and this one had none.

Its end was scheduled. So, there was no sense starting it.

Yet … they were connected. She couldn't explain it, but she knew they were connected. The connection tugged her toward him, step by step. As if her walk followed a line stretching from her to him and back again. Possibly a line of something that conducted electricity, from the way she felt.

As long as she remembers they're just ships passing in the night and not to get tangled up … Are you getting entangled?

Of course not.

Just … connected.

Ed said something to the group he was with, and turned toward her. She forgot about Lydia's voice in her head. She didn't care about

Angela's narrowed eyes. She focused on Ed.

He was going to take her hands in his. Maybe take her in his arms—

But as they met, before they could touch, Henri was there beside her again.

"Ah, so, this is the so-famous gentleman from Wyoming," he said with a flirty smile. "We weren't properly introduced before."

CHAPTER FIVE

Friday evening

"Henri—"

Ed caught several layers of warnings to her friend in Donna's voice, along with exasperation.

"Yes, yes, I know, you want me to go away. But if you think for a moment, and if you see—*without* looking around, thank you very much—that our not-so-sweet Charity is considering which knife to throw at you first, you will come to thank your dear Henri for making this a threesome. So to speak."

Donna sighed in acceptance of her friend's concern, which put Ed on alert. He had no problem turning aside Angela's less than subtle advances, a skill learned while rodeoing, but if the older woman posed any threat to Donna, he wanted to hear more.

"Ed, this is Henri LeFleur. Don't believe the name or accent. He's as American as we are. Henri, this is Ed Currick, who will not fall for your shtick. And, if you try to use Ed to make Brad jealous, I will *not* be happy." She propped her hands on her hips. "Do you understand?"

"Oh, Donna, so much distrust in one so young and lovely is not becoming. Causes wrinkles." Henri gestured to a spot between his eyebrows. "Besides, as it happens, our young Ed here has already met Brad. Now, aren't you sorry you wronged me? And the conversation was entirely innocent. Entirely just us guys."

He dropped to bass on the last three words, drawing a chuckle from Ed.

He'd felt the tension between Henri and Brad when Lydia had

introduced them, and he was pretty sure he'd have figured it out even if Donna hadn't given it away.

She hadn't wanted him caught off guard. Or did she fear he'd be shocked? Either way, she'd been looking out for him. That felt good.

"What did you talk about?" Donna asked, clearly considering him the more reliable source.

"The bus breakdown, theater construction, the tour's schedule, and pro football."

"Pro football," Henri repeated with a little shiver. Then he perked up. "Ah, there is estimable Maudie, along with Lydia. The reinforcements needed for the job of protective coloring I have borne on my own. I beckon and, yes, they begin to come this way."

"I have no idea what you're talking about," Donna said. But she flashed Ed a look, and he suspected the one he returned ratcheted up the heat a degree or ten.

"*Please.*" Henri drew it out until they both looked at him. "You are making me blush with these glances. What a shame our Angel of Death hovers and the music isn't right, or you two could at least dance. These hotly longing looks are generally thought acceptable on a dance floor."

"Sorry, can't dance," Ed said.

"Oh, no," protested Henri, "your line should be 'I Won't Dance.' "

"I would if I could, at least with Donna, but I can't."

"No, no, it must be *won't* dance," insisted Henri, looking from one to the other with significance. "There is a song 'I Won't Dance' in one of those Fred Astaire and Ginger Rogers movies our Donna so loves."

Ed saw brighter color seeping into her cheeks. She knew what was coming. With more interest, he turned to listen to Henri.

"And according to the song, the reason Fred won't dance with Ginger is not because he can't, but because it would be far too tempting to do something else entirely. Yes, I think the line fits this situation, perfectly. If he puts his arms around her, it *won't* be to dance."

"Were you really talking to Brad about football?" she asked Ed. She'd decided to ignore the topic of Henri's outrageous banter. "Brad hardly talks to anybody. Usually just barks."

They'd filled plates at the buffet, then found a quiet, dim corner well back from the party and its chatter. To enjoy their meal in peace, she'd said.

They'd long finished eating, and neither made a move to leave their seclusion.

"Yep, really was. Also about your upcoming schedule. He seems to be looking forward to your show being in San Francisco for Christmas."

"San Francisco?" She focused on the holiday-themed napkin she was twisting in her hands. It showed two red bells, sporting gold bows against boughs of greenery. "I just knew we'd be in California."

She hadn't looked at the schedule since Thanksgiving. Except for one specific element.

"How much longer are you here?"

That was the one element she'd checked. Earlier today. Trying to pretend she didn't know why she was interested.

"We leave a week from Sunday, right after the show." At its most generous count, ten days away. Aiming for offhand, she asked, "When does the stock show end?"

"Sunday." She started to smile at the serendipity, then he added, "Day after tomorrow."

"Oh." She swallowed. "When are you leaving?"

"Supposed to check out Monday."

No.

For a long moment of suspended heartbeat and held breath that was the only thought to come. Then more rushed in.

No. That's too fast. No time at all. He can't leave so fast. It can't be over. Not yet. Not before they'd even—

"What about your schedule for the rest of the—run, you call it?"

he asked.

She blinked. Shaken by her own thoughts. Trying to get her mind to grapple with the simple information to answer him.

"We have two-a-days tomorrow and Sunday. Then we're off Monday."

But his stock show ended tomorrow. He'd be gone before she had her day off. Gone before—

Before they made love.

Yes.

That was what was in her mind. In her bloodstream.

Making love with Ed Currick.

This man she barely knew. A relationship whose ending was as immutable as the date on a calendar.

She shot a look at him, and found his attention fully on her.

Oh, God. She wanted to make love with him.

"The, uh, the rest of next week should be more routine. It's a saying that the company lives for Week Twos. We have more time off, we can explore the city we're in or—" She steered around "or." "Then two-a-days Saturday, before Sunday…"

…before Sunday's finale and departure.

He'd be long gone. Back to Knighton, Wyoming. Back to the ranch that had been in his family for generations.

She didn't want to think of moving-ons. Not hers, not his.

She dropped her head, smoothing the napkin out on her thigh, carefully ironing the creases and wrinkles with her fingers.

"Christmas is coming, huh?" he said, looking over her shoulder at the napkin. He sounded a little forced. He tapped a fingertip to the greenery behind the bells. The touch gathered heat as it traveled through the napkin, her slacks and into her skin. "Looks like snowberry. We have some on the Slash-C."

He'd leave so soon, return to his ranch, to where they had snowberry for real, not just as illustrations on napkins.

He'd leave.

She'd never see him again. Never…

But they had now.

They had *now.*

They had *tonight.*

They had to have tonight.

Could she do it?

"Snowberry. Sounds like the perfect plant for Christmas," she said, brightly. She knew she said it brightly, because she hit the exact intonation she'd used for Ado Annie in "Oklahoma" in college, when the director said he wanted *brightly,* then called it perfect. "My favorite time of the year. I bet you decorate with snowberry."

If she stretched up, touched her lips to his...

She ducked her head, the wanting and the uncertainty both too much, and said, with every bit of Ado Annie brightness she possessed, "I love Christmas decorations, don't you?"

"Uh, Christmas lights are nice." It sounded like the vocal equivalent of someone feeling his way through fog.

"They're wonderful," she agreed, ever more brightly. "On the houses and shops and trees. All lit up so whole blocks glow. Just wonderful."

"Don't see that much in Wyoming. Lights are more spread out. Every year some neighbors put lights on this tree, using a whole lot of extension cords. I don't think they can even see it from their place, but if you drive by, or if I'm riding that section, there it is, all the colors shining, out there all by itself."

"That's ... that's wonderful, Ed." She wanted to kiss him. She wanted ... him. "A wreath on the front door."

"What?"

He sounded off-balance at her blurted words. Thank God, she wasn't alone.

"A wreath on the front door. That's what tells me Christmas is coming at home. Not made from snowberry though." Her brightness was nearly too much to bear. "Now it's your turn."

"A bow on the truck, I guess."

Curiosity dialed the brightness in her voice back toward reality.

"You put a bow on your truck? Inside or out?"

"On the front grill mostly. Sometimes on the rearview mirror. Mom puts them on."

"I like that." Maybe she would have something in common with his mother. Not that they'd ever meet. "Mailing cards to friends," she said quickly.

"Calling Merry Christmas at anybody you pass by on the road."

"Carolers going door to door."

"Doors too far apart. So barn dance where everybody sings together."

"Like what happened when our bus broke down. That's nice."

"Yeah, it is. In the old days, it took so long to get anywhere, people came from all over and stayed a night or two. They'd dance 'til dawn on the last day, then start traveling. Now folks come for the evening. Except, one year when I was a kid, there was a storm, and everybody stayed over, and all us kids wanted to do it every year. But it's not very practical."

"I suppose not."

"You're not wishing for the old days are you?" he asked. "Because forget the nostalgia, it was a heck of a lot of work."

"I know. And, no, I'm not wishing for the old days. Not all parts of them, only … community, I guess."

"We've got that in Knighton. Suppose you have to when there aren't a lot of people. Most folks are pretty self-reliant, but some jobs need more hands, so it's good to have neighbors to count on. I never thought about it as anything special until college, when I realized my life had been different from some of the other kids'."

They had tonight.

"Where is Knighton?"

"Eastern slope of the Big Horns—Big Horn Mountains," he elaborated, apparently reading her blankness. "You know anything about Wyoming?"

She searched her memory. "Sort of square. Uh, Yellowstone Park? Cheyenne?"

"Not near either one," he said cheerfully. "Yellowstone's the northwest corner. If you cut the box of Wyoming into four, Cheyenne's in the southeast quadrant. Knighton would be on the west side of the northeast quarter, 'bout halfway down."

"What's it like?"

She wanted him to keep talking, while she considered something she had never before considered. Making love with a man she couldn't have a future with. A man who would leave when this weekend was over.

Tonight ... Would she dare...?

"Not much there."

"There must be something there. Tell me."

"Okay. There's a main street—called Main Street. Buildings like the library and courthouse, a couple of churches, and what's now an elementary school are from the '20s, built from native stone. Then there's the cafe and other places built of wood.

"The town started with a log building at a crossroads. A sort of bar—what they called a roadhouse in the early days. Pretty rough. Cowboys and rustlers and cardsharks, all together. A few other businesses started to serve the roadhouse's customers. Livery stable, general store, and a bawdy house run by the ancestor of one of the town's most upright citizens." He grinned. "Everybody acts like nobody knows, but everybody does."

Despite the distraction of her other thoughts, he'd caught her attention.

"As more folks moved in, there was pressure to make it a proper town. One night, the roadhouse and bawdy house mysteriously burned—no injuries, and surprisingly little property loss, since the furnishings were out in the road for some odd reason." He winked, and she grinned. "The next day, construction started on the building that's the cafe to this day, and the woman who ran the bawdy house and her girls were respectable—just like that. Overnight."

"Everyone accepted them?"

"Sure. There weren't many women around. They couldn't afford to shun any. After a while, there wasn't a family that didn't have a connection to one of Miss Jean's girls."

"Including your family?"

"Oh, no, none of Miss Jean's girls were in my family tree. Miss Jean herself. Married my grandfather's uncle."

She laughed. A genuine, true laugh.

Their ships would pass. He would return to his Knighton and his ranch. She would move on to wherever next. But they had right now. Right this instant.

That had to be enough.

He put his arm around her, and she forgot everything else.

"There you two are," Lydia said, making a production out of coming around a back curtain. She'd have made less noise with a set of cymbals. "I'd've knocked, but there's no door. C'mon, the bus is about to leave."

"We'll walk back," Donna said quickly.

They had tonight.

"No, we won't. Too late." Ed stood, holding out his hand to her as if she'd need help getting out of the chair.

"It's not—"

"Not going to have you out on the streets this time of night with only me to look out for you."

"Ed—"

"Donna."

Looking up at him, she knew they were riding back in the bus, just as they'd eaten at the diner.

She thought about that on the bus ride.

Ed Currick was mostly a very easy-going person. Until he encountered something he felt was the right thing to do.

Or not the right thing to do.

So how would he react to her trying to get him into bed?

CHAPTER SIX

Saturday

"Flat."

Brad appeared out of nowhere and shot the single word at her as she'd trailed the others to the dressing room after the matinee.

"No way. When—?" she started indignantly. Then she realized she didn't recall a single note of the numbers she'd performed.

"Whole thing, beginning to end. No oomph at all."

He'd meant her performance. She released her shoulders back into a slump. "Sorry, Brad. I'll do better tonight."

"Better."

He might have simply repeated her word. More likely it was an order. Possibly a threat. He was gone before she felt any obligation to find out which. She didn't particularly care, because—

"He wasn't here this afternoon, was he?"

Donna's head came up at Maudie's voice. The older woman stepped forward from a shadow.

"Who wasn't—?"

Maudie stopped the charade with a shake of her head. "Ed Currick of the Slash-C Ranch in Knighton, Wyoming. Is that because you had sex with him last night or because you didn't?"

"*Maudie!*"

"Are you shocked I know about sex? Or that you want it. No, no, don't answer. Go get out of your makeup and into your clothes, and come to my room down that corridor."

"I'm going to get some food with the girls—"

"You need rest before tonight's show, and reasonable discussion. Not chattering. Now, do what I say. Fifteen minutes, I will expect you."

Maudie's room was surely as dingy and tattered as the rest of backstage, but that wasn't what Donna saw after knocking and being invited to enter.

Warmth and comfort and ease.

A muted paisley throw formed a backdrop—pinned to a clothesline, Donna eventually realized. An oriental patterned rug warmed a rectangle of floor. A small lamp's glow contrasted with the sharp makeup lights of the dressing room and with the dimness of the rest of backstage.

"Maudie, this is … Where did you get all this?"

"My special things travel along, tucked in corners."

The tiny space reminded Donna both of a reading nook in her parents' house and the cleverly outfitted milieu of a fortune-teller she and friends had visited in New Orleans.

Donna realized she'd never been to Maudie's cubbyholes in any of the theaters they'd been in. Maudie always came to them.

"If the theater's your home—onstage or backstage—you'd best make yourself comfortable." Maudie sat in a chair draped by another colored throw. "Now, sit, and have some tea and something to eat. Chicken, fruit, a few carrots—not too many, mind—and tea are best between a matinee and evening performance. Never fish."

"I know about orange juice and grapefruit juice, but I never heard about fish. Is it bad for the voice, too?"

"Bad for the rest of the people backstage—the smell."

Donna chuckled, and sat on a sofa. Stage sofas were never this soft because it made it difficult to get out of them on cue. She looked more closely and saw an extra cushion on the sofa. "Yours?"

"Of course. Now have some chicken."

Donna ate, suddenly hungry.

"There is a charge for this meal, Donna. Your young man did not come this afternoon, and I ask you why?"

"It had absolutely nothing to do with … sex."

"You did not have sex with him last night?"

Sex? They'd barely kissed.

While a crowd from the company had ostentatiously held the elevator door for her, he'd kissed her goodnight almost chastely.

So much for their having the night.

"No. And—"

"But you want to have sex with him."

"I want to—" Almost too late she saw how changing *have sex* to *make love* might cause more misunderstanding. "Yes."

Maudie let out a little breath that sounded … satisfied? Why?

"So what was the cause of his missing this show?"

"It's not like he's been to every show," Donna started defensively. Maudie simply looked at her over her tea cup. "He's at the stock show—livestock show."

Words tumbled out of her about Ed, his family, the Slash-C, and Wyoming. She said nothing about her feelings. Or her wonderings about his.

When she stopped, Maudie poured more tea. Only with the cup half emptied did she say, "Brad was right, you were flat this afternoon."

Stricken as she had not been when Brad said it, Donna had no response.

"Tonight will be better. You needed the right food and you have had it. Now you need a vocal rest. So you will listen, and I will talk. What so many young people do not understand is they must love this—" Maudie's gesture took in their cozy space, yet called to mind the wider realm of backstage. "As much as the singing and dancing. Indeed, more."

"More?"

"Add up your time onstage, then add up your time on all the rest. The traveling. The waiting. The checks. The wardrobe calls. The meetings. The command performances at opening night parties. The maneuvering." Maudie shot her a look. "That's your real life when you're in the theater. Not singing and dancing."

"Rehearsal is. Rehearsal's the best—"

"Vocal rest," the older woman ordered. Donna shut her mouth. "Being onstage—performance or rehearsal—is the tip of the iceberg. All the rest of it are layers upon layers of ice building up from the bottom to hold you high enough to be seen above the surface. That's being onstage. Take Angela."

"Angela?"

"Our Charity," Maudie said, as if, instead of repeating the name because she didn't see how she fit this conversation, Donna needed an introduction. "She revels in it. Especially the maneuvering. If there were no singing, no dancing, no acting, but still her name was in Playbill, people coming to applaud her, and, most of all, the backstage dramas to put her atop the heap, she would be perfectly satisfied. She has been that way from the start."

Donna's eyes widened.

Maudie nodded. "I was there on her first road company. She worked very hard. Got herself noticed, too. Two entirely different things, you know. Easy to do one without the other. But Angela knows where she wants to go. Nothing gets in her way."

The older woman's look gave those final words added significance. A warning to not get in Angela's way? Or a warning that Donna needed more of that intensity?

"One of the principals in that company was an up-and-comer. A lot of talent, a lot of sparkle. Started hearing rumors she was being looked at for bigger things. She and Angela hit it off. Got so you didn't see one without the other. Except one time, we had a couple days travel, and Angela was nowhere to be found. Nobody knew where she was, including her good friend.

"Angela comes back, looking like a cat who's feasted on a canary. Three weeks later, Angela's gone to take the lead in that first TV series she got so famous for, one where she was the sexy daughter of …

Who was he?"

"The nation's only crime-solving governor. He signed the laws and then enforced them," Donna recited from the intro to one of her favorite shows growing up.

"Right. So Angela had the lead, and her great friend was mad as fire. Seems she'd been scheduled to test for the role on our next break. Angela got there first."

"Angela stole the role?"

Maudie shook her head. "No role belongs to anyone, so no stealing. All I know is her friend said the only person she told about the audition was Angela. The friendship ended. Still, her friend did okay for herself, then retired to marry a doctor. And Angela didn't stay up.

"The TV show got her a couple movies. Didn't work," Maudie was saying. "Two more series didn't stick. Then the one about a school for clowns was on its way out. She tried for Broadway. No deal. But she fit okay for taking this on the road. So here she is…"

From Donna's standpoint, lead in a touring company would be a dream. From Angela's it must be less impressive.

"Now the word is she's angling for another TV show. That's the way of this business. It's like climbing a mountain. Sometimes you make good progress. Sometimes you fall far enough to break your neck if you're not lucky. You've got to be willing to go anywhere you can get a hold—up, down, sideways—just to stay on the mountain. It's the ones who get a thrill from that who're suited to this life." She studied Donna. "You're like her in a lot of ways."

"Like *Angela*?"

"*Tch*. Not Angela. Theresa."

"Who's Theresa?"

"Who's Theresa? Who've I been talking about all this time."

"But…" Donna swallowed the protest that Maudie had never mentioned the other woman's name. Then voiced a different protest. "I'm not going to quit and marry a doctor."

The wrinkles on Maudie's face rearranged into a smile. "I'd be greatly surprised if you marry a doctor. Greatly surprised."

That night at the theater, Ed heard people during the break—interval, they called it—talking about other members of the cast. How could they see anyone else on the stage for the beaming brightness of Donna?

He wasn't sure he grasped details of the show he'd seen four nights in a row, because he only watched her. When other actors took over, he remembered her every move, every smile, every gesture.

Course, that happened when she wasn't on the stage, too.

He'd stumbled through meetings at the stock show, feeling as if his words came out jumbled like a puzzle in the Sunday comics. So he'd concentrated on listening, trying to hear, hoping to remember. Thinking about her all the time.

And now, seeing her, like he was seeing her for the first time.

Only it wasn't like the first time, because he wasn't seeing the woman he'd spotted across the lobby. He was seeing the star she would be.

She *would* be a star. There was no doubt. Her spirit and talent would take her as far as she wanted to go.

Broadway. That's where she'd want to be.

Not the Slash-C in Knighton, Wyoming. About as far from Broadway as it got. Not only no stages, but no audiences.

The one place he belonged. The one place…

He drove one fist into his other palm, and hunched over in the theater seat.

How could he ever ask her to give up her dream for his?

How could he even want her to give up her dream for his?

How could he not want her dream for her?

He couldn't. Right down the line, that was the answer. He couldn't.

And that left him … What?

He should leave. Leave right now. She'd wonder for a while, but she'd get over it. She'd forget—

"Excuse me."

His head jerked up at the voice of the woman trying to return to her seat. He stood to let her by.

"Thank you. Are you okay, dear?"

"Yes'm."

She paused a moment, then took her seat.

He remained standing. He could leave right now. Cut his losses. Make a clean break. He should—

The lights flicked a final time. The orchestra struck up.

He sat.

And when the curtain rose, he watched only one person.

Ed was there inside the stage door after the evening performance.

"Grover said to come in. Said to call a taxi from here so you didn't have to walk back to the hotel. Thought we'd eat there."

"No taxi. I want to walk. We'll find someplace along the way."

"Sure you want to walk? Two-a-days are tough on the legs."

"Listen to you, Mr. Showbiz." Donna smiled, and he smiled back. After a long moment, she swallowed. Then someone bumped into her, with a hurried *Sorry*, knocking her away from him. "Yes, I want to walk."

They took a different route tonight, quickly separating from those headed to the diner. Perfect. She needed time to work on him.

She turned toward a shop window as if looking at it had been her reason for stopping.

There was so little time left.

"Hungry?" he asked from beside her.

Only then did she realize she'd stopped in front of a bakery window. It featured glittery snowflakes suspended over velvet wrapped boxes. "Guess I am."

"Figured you had to be near starving, because you've barely said a word."

She smiled at his teasing.

"Want to try there?" He pointed across the street.

The narrow restaurant served heavenly Mexican food, and no one spoke English.

It was as if a bubble settled around the two of them. She talked about her childhood. He asked about her family, her brother in Chicago, her sister still at home. She asked about his. His father was a lawyer, he had an older sister, married and living in Montana. They talked about college. He spoke about his ranch, the Slash-C … and when he did, he was an artist talking about the core of his passion.

"Spending so much time on the ranch, it must be wonderful to get away. To come to someplace like Denver and—"

"I'm not in Denver to get away. I came to learn more about cross-breeding. Couldn't connect with these people if I stay on the Slash-C."

"But you must be having fun here, outside the stock show. Sight-seeing, and—No? Then what were you doing?"

"Spent all day at the stock show. Meals with folks from the stock show. Then back to the hotel and read in my room."

"Read?"

"About changes in breeding. That's why I came back to the hotel Wednesday afternoon—to get an article I'd promised to another rancher."

"Ed, that's awful. Your first time—"

"Not my first time in Denver. I've been to a fair number of cities. Guess you could say this isn't my first rodeo." The humor glint was back. "Rodeo took me around a fair bit, college and after."

"So, you got to know these cities then? Explored and enjoyed them?"

"I wasn't there to explore and enjoy. I was there to rodeo. Kept my focus on that."

She frowned. "Focus can go too far. You need to have fun."

"What makes you think breeding cattle isn't fun?"

He waggled his eyebrows, and she squinted fiercely. "You're a tease, Ed Currick. I'm not going to take anything you say seriously ever again."

The waiter came up to the table with the bill then, but Ed held her look.

"Oh, there're some things I say you should take very seriously."

Donna gave a guilty start when Ed squeezed her hand. She'd been thinking about Thursday night's kiss, and wondering about tonight.

"What's that you're humming?" he asked. "It's not from the show. I know those." He hummed a couple bars. Not well. It took a moment for her to catch the tune.

"Oh. 'Let's Call the Whole Thing Off' from a Fred Astaire-Ginger Rogers movie."

"How come you know all these old movies?"

"Mom saw them with *her* mom. Now, when they're on TV we make popcorn, sing the songs, speak the lines, and do some of the dancing. When I was little, I pestered Mom and Dad for lessons so I could dance like Ginger Rogers and that started the whole thing."

"A family legacy."

"Yes. You might know this song. He says po-tay-to, and she says pah-ta-to—or maybe the other way around. And to-may-to, to-mah-to. Then comes the title line, 'Let's Call The Whole Thing Off.' "

"Yeah, that's familiar."

"But a couple lines later the song says they'd be heartbroken if they call it off."

"Oh, yeah? Then what?"

"Um. They decide not to—call it off, I mean."

His eyes darkened with heat. "Sounds like a good call."

She looked away. "Works in the movie."

They'd walked several more blocks before she said, "You're back to being silent."

He got that solemn look he'd had before they left the restaurant. "Don't want to scare you."

"You just did."

He smiled quickly. "Fair enough."

"Why would you scare me?"

"Because it scares me."

"What does?"

"How I feel about you."

"Oh." At least that's what she tried to say, but it had no breath behind it, only the forming of her lips. He looked at her mouth, and she felt her diaphragm contract, and heat sweep down from it to her belly, leaving a trail of sparks.

"You looked like this that first day," she started, without any knowledge that's what she was going to say. "With your mouth smiling, but your eyes so serious—not unhappy, but intense."

"First moment I saw you in the lobby. I saw…"

"What?"

"You," he said, the rasp of his voice like a touch on her nerve-endings.

Yet there was more he wasn't telling her. And she wasn't asking.

He lowered his head. "I saw you," he repeated.

His mouth on hers was neither chaste nor soft.

She gasped at the power of the demand his lips made, and his tongue swept into her mouth with a stroke she felt in her core.

Her knees half sagged. His arm around her back not only held her, but brought her even tighter against him.

She brushed a palm across his cheek on the way to wrapping her arms around his neck, and felt a jolt through him, and marveled. Such a simple touch.

But if it was so simple, then why was she spinning … spinning … with nothing real around her to anchor her and keep the spin from consuming her balance.

Something firm against her back stopped the spinning. Except for in her head.

Oh. A wall. A wall was behind her. He'd brought them into a re-cessed doorway. It was dimmer here. Warmer out of the wind.

No, not warmer. Hot. *Hot.*

His hand under her sweater and shirt. Up her side. The heat of that touch. So very hot. And so close. But not…

She turned into it. Yes. *Yes.*

Her fingers opening his coat, his shirt, seeking him.

His hands holding her, cupping her. Unhooking. Then pushing aside the remaining fabric, the softest scratch of lace across her beaded, sensitized nipple. Then … oh, yes.

"Yes."

CHAPTER SEVEN

Friday night

No.

As desperately as he wanted to … No.

Ranching would send a pessimistic man around the bend. But ranching also required pragmatism and an ability to face facts squarely.

He'd faced the facts here. Even if he hadn't been able to walk away yet.

Donna wanted what she had up on that stage and that was one thing he couldn't give her.

So why hadn't he left? Why wasn't he ending this right now?

It would hurt less than letting it go on, wouldn't it? Less for him and for her. Sense said it would. And he'd always had good sense.

She moved against him.

Through layers of clothing still covering them, he felt his body surge with the need to find that spot in her that would hold him. Hold him so rightly. He knew that.

But it wasn't only that. It was what he'd seen in her eyes that first moment in the lobby of the hotel. What he hadn't told her. Might never tell another living soul.

She moved again.

Between them they had created their own cocoon of heat. If there were nothing between them—

"We have to stop, Donna." He drew back as far as he could bear.

She followed. Her lips brushed one corner of his. "Do we?"

"Yes."

"We, uh … I mean, I have a roommate, but your room."

He groaned.

"Is that a yes?" Her teasing didn't quite come off.

Because she wasn't sure. She wanted to, but she wasn't sure.

"No," he said.

She ducked her head, and the shift in position allowed cold to sweep into their cocoon. He drew her flush against him, and kissed her. Delved his tongue inside her mouth, and kissed her with more power and intent than he'd allowed himself before, until the stupid limits of the human body required him to release her long enough to suck in oxygen.

"No," he repeated, partly to himself.

"Your mouth says no, but your body says something else." Again, her teasing had a hitch in it.

"My body says I'm a damned idiot. But my mind's connected to my mouth." He looked down at her, knowing she would see what he felt, at least a little.

And as he knew it would, it made her draw back. Just a little. Just enough.

He tugged at her top, not bothering with the bra, but pulling the hem down on her shirt and sweater so she was covered, then grabbed the sides of her coat and wrapped them tightly around her, careful not to brush her body beneath the coat.

That let cold air flood in against his heated chest, and regions barely contained by his jeans, but he needed that. He needed it bad.

"Ed," she said abruptly. "Where were you sitting tonight?"

"What?"

"Where were you sitting in the theater?"

She made it sound like something important, though he didn't see it. "Left side, about halfway back."

"Oh." A second of relaxing, then she tightened up again. "Wait. Left side from front of house, or left from the stage?"

"Left from where I came in with other people."

"Oh."

There was more in those two letters than he could hope to under-stand. "Why?"

She ignored that. "And last night?"

"What's this about?"

"Last night?" she repeated.

"Near the center aisle. Tenth row I think."

"Were you at the matinee Thursday?"

"No."

She gave a sort of groan. But it didn't sound bad enough to keep him from his more immediate concerns.

"C'mon, I'm getting you back to the hotel. Back to *your* room."

CHAPTER EIGHT

Sunday

Last night, they'd parted once again with an audience at the elevator. This time not even kissing. Instead, a long look acknowledged memories of really kissing each other, and not chastely at all.

They'd agreed to have brunch before she left for the theater for today's matinee and he attended the stock show's closing day.

He was eating a hearty breakfast. Eggs and sausage and potatoes and tomatoes and biscuits. A cowboy breakfast, he'd said.

Had to on a ranch, he'd explained. Talking about early rising to tend to animals that didn't believe in sleeping in. Talking about how the first break of the day was to refuel a body that had already had more demands on it than many people experienced in a week.

"We seem to spend all our time eating," he said.

"Not a lot of free time first week, and with all the shows…" She shrugged.

"You need the fuel, too."

"Uh-huh."

She picked up a triangle of toast. He was right. Closing day of the stock show was not all that would keep them apart today. Two performances, too. Was there a chance they could be together tonight before he left tomorrow?

Closing day … *Leaving tomorrow.*

She put the toast down and closed her eyes. She'd cried last night. Lying in bed, tears slipping down the side of her face and into her pillow. Not knowing if she was crying because she wasn't making love with him. Or because he was the kind of man who would try to protect her.

And wondering which of those elements was behind her sensing where he was in the theater each time he'd been there.

No, not *sensing. Knowing.* Like a plant turning to the sun. Like a plant about to be cut off from the sun forev—

"Donna?"

She pretended great interest in spreading grape jelly on her toast. She didn't like grape jelly. "Uh-huh?"

"I'll stay a few a days longer if you'd like me to."

Her head snapped up.

If she'd like him to?

He blinked, as if facing a bright light, but didn't look away. And it didn't make sense anyway, because *he* was the sun, not her. Oh, hell, what did that stuff matter now?

"That's wonderful, Ed. How long? How long can you stay?"

"As long as you're here."

"Really?" Her heart tripped, then sprinted ahead. There would be hours and hours together. Not just snatches, but all of tomorrow, and then whole afternoons…

"But … but you wanted to get back to the Slash-C."

"I don't know if I *could* leave while you're here."

He didn't sound entirely happy, but he was staying. She'd concentrate on that certainty, put aside the fogginess of what he might be thinking.

"I thought Monday we'd drive up to the mountains," he said. "Spend the day, let you see them up close."

"Oh, Ed, that's so thoughtful of you."

"Good. We'll leave as early as——"

"No, wait. I have something else I'd rather do. I mean if it's okay. Would you take me to the stock show? Unless—Are there places in Denver you haven't had a chance to see? I was reading about—but not tomorrow. Tomorrow I'd like to learn about ranching—at least cattle. So would you take me to the stock show? I know this is the last day, but will everything be gone by tomorrow?"

His brows drew together, as if he were viewing something he hadn't seen before. "I guess not. But they'll be breaking things down, packing up, pulling out."

"Perfect! You can see so many things when we're striking."

"Striking?"

"Closing up the show for a move. Definitely see lots when we're packing—or unpacking. You see the real workings and—what?"

His expression was shifting to that smile she loved, with an added dash of humor. "I never considered that. Don't know if you're right or not, but I suppose we'll find out tomorrow. But are you sure? You haven't seen the Rockies."

"There'll be more mountains." But she would never have another chance to spend a day with Ed Currick in his world.

I'll stay a few a days longer if you'd like me to.

Good God, what had possessed him?

Like he needed to ask. She had. Sitting across from her, and knowing that even if she'd said, "No, go on home and get started on being without me forever," he wouldn't have gone.

I don't know if I could leave while you're here.

That was the truth of it.

He sat in the lobby phone booth. No use putting it off any longer. He placed the call.

His father answered with the usual, "Slash-C."

He felt a constriction in his throat, immediate, and completely unexpected.

"Dad. It's Ed."

"Ed. Your mother will be sorry to have missed your call."

"I wanted to let you both know I won't be home tomorrow night. I'm, uh, going to stay longer in Denver."

"Learning more than you expected, eh? Or are you teaching the folks there."

"Little of both, I guess."

"Good, good. So, when should I tell your mother to expect you?"

"A week from Monday. Not sure of the time."

"A week," his father repeated slowly.

"Yeah. Tell Mom to call Pauly Trudeau or Hem Robertson to help her out. Or both. They'd appreciate the offseason work. I'll pay their wages when I get back."

"I'll tell her. Anything else you want me to tell her?"

"No. That covers it." He was suddenly glad his mother hadn't taken this call. She wouldn't have been satisfied without a lot more information.

"Ed, you're a grown man, as I'm always telling your mother, so … Is there anything—are *you* okay?"

"Yes, sir, I am."

"Are you okay with money to stay another week?"

"Yes, sir."

There was a pause. "Okay, then. Call if you need anything. Or … if your plans change again."

"I will."

They said their farewells, hung up. But Ed didn't move.

If his plans changed again.

As if he were in charge of any of this.

It was more like he was a calf, well and truly roped. Being drawn slowly, inexorably toward the fire where the branding iron waited.

Only this calf wanted the fire, wanted to wear the brand, even as it dragged back on the rope. Hoping it wouldn't burn quite as much as it knew it would.

And knowing that then he'd be let loose. But not free.

After the evening performance, Donna came around the corner of the hallway, able to see the stage door now. Before her mind recognized Ed, something else in her did—her breath caught, and her tired muscles lightened.

"Well, well, the faithful swain remains faithful," murmured Henri from beside her, then added darkly. "So far as you know. Or think you know, because men are lying bastards."

By which Donna understood that the rumor about Henri and Brad's latest fight was true. She made a sound meant to combine acknowledgment and sympathy, but without much attention because all of hers was pinned on the tall, broad-shouldered figure wearing the cowboy hat.

Henri's sound was one of disgust as he peeled off and went into the wardrobe room. She barely noticed.

Ed had his head bowed as he listened intently to something Maudie was telling him. He held a paper while she stabbed a finger at a point on it.

Maudie spotted her, said something to Ed. He folded the paper and slipped it inside his open jacket.

"What are you two conspiring over?" she teased, as she came close enough to wrap both hands around his arm. His opposite hand came up and clasped over hers, as if to secure her hold on him.

"Nothing." He didn't meet her eyes, even as his hand tightened.

"Maudie—?" But the older woman was walking away, heading toward her cubbyhole, and Grover was beside her. So much for attending the door.

She turned to Ed. Before she got in a question, he said, "Temperature's dropped. We'll get a cab."

She started to protest, then decided a cab was a good idea. A really good idea. It would get them to the hotel, and his room, faster.

"Where would you like to eat?" He held the door for her.

Cold rushed around her, inside her, licking up her legs under the coat's hem, burrowing inside the cuffs, slapping her face.

"I'm not hungry. Let's just go to the hotel." The sooner they got to the hotel, the sooner she could seduce him, once and for all. *Let's just go to bed.* That's what she wanted.

"No supper? You feeling okay?"

"Mmm-hmm. Maudie gave me the perfect meal between performances."

He used one long arm to wrap her to his side so his body protected her from the worst of the cold as they came out of the alley. He raised his other arm to signal to a taxi sitting down the block. Even in the short time it took for the taxi to arrive and to get in it, she felt as if her face had iced in place.

The taxi's interior was cozy by contrast, and Ed radiated heat beside her, especially when he put his arm around her and she snuggled close.

"What were you talking about with Maudie?" she asked when he'd finished telling the driver where they were going.

He put his hand over hers where it rested on his chest. "You're freezing." He opened a button of his jacket and slid her hand in.

Ahh, delicious.

She flexed her fingers, feeling the muscle beneath his shirt. She would see his strength uncovered tonight. Stripped … although the idea of taking her own clothes off made her curl into a tighter ball to hold onto the warmth.

"Maudie?" she repeated, before a yawn overtook her.

"Nothing much. Why don't you close your eyes? You've gotta be beat with all these shows."

She yawned again. Had to be nerves. Though he was right she had reason to be beat. Seven performances in four days, the party, minimal sleep. The lack of sleep was his fault, of course. But that would end tonight.

She wouldn't lie awake thinking about him tonight. Not once she'd seduced him.

Maybe she would close her eyes. Just for a little.

He considered carrying her in from the taxi, let her keep sleeping. But it would have raised eyebrows. Along with making it even harder to ignore how much he wanted to ask her—drag her, beg her—back to his room.

She gave him a sleepy smile as they entered the elevator. Some might think the yawn that swallowed it dented the smile's sexiness. Not him.

He fought a mighty battle with himself in the two quick breaths before he leaned over and hit two buttons—his floor and her floor.

At her floor, they crossed the elevator threshold together, took a couple steps, then he pivoted, catching the door just in time, and re-entered the elevator alone.

She was another yard down the hallway before she realized, looking back at him, then at the numbers on the doors nearby in confusion.

"I thought—Your room's on the same floor?"

"No. You get some sleep."

"But—"

"Go on now. If I hold the door much longer the alarm will go off, and people'll be mad."

She stood there, looking back at him. He cursed under his breath, let the door go and stepped out before it closed.

"Where's your key?"

She handed it over, and he saw the number was a couple doors away. He guided her there.

"Oh, good. You're coming in," she said as he opened the door.

She was so tired she'd forgotten the existence of Lydia, who'd return shortly.

"No. Go in, Donna." He put the key in her unresisting hand, and nudged her into the room. "We have all of tomorrow."

Before he ran out of willpower, he closed the door on himself.

Sometimes being a gentleman was a pain in the ass—and another part of his anatomy.

Yeah, things were definitely harder, he thought later, grimacing as he cupped his head in his interlocked fingers and stared at the ceiling.

Couldn't possibly get any harder.

CHAPTER NINE

Monday

"Tell me more about Wyoming," Donna demanded.

While they ate breakfast, then drove his pickup to the grounds, she'd peppered him with questions about the stock show. Now that they'd parked at a distance necessitated by livestock trucks clogging close-in spots, she'd shifted focus.

"It's home."

"Some people hate their home."

He looked at her. "You?"

"No. I love my family, and the house I grew up in. And Indiana's great, it's just…"

"Just?" he prompted.

"I think I always knew I was headed for someplace else."

Without turning his head, he cut a look toward her. When she'd gotten to the word *headed*, he'd fully expected the rest of the sentence to be *to Broadway*. Was he fooling himself thinking that a couple days ago it would have been?

Yeah, he probably was.

As if to confirm his assessment, she gave herself a small shake. "But we're not talking about me, we're talking about Wyoming."

"Go right ahead then," he invited with a grin. "Talk."

"Edward—"

She interrupted herself mid-scold. "What's your middle name?"

"David."

"Thank you for the cue."

She picked up where she'd left off:

"—David Currick, don't be difficult. Tell me more about Wyoming."

"Prairie in the east, Rockies in the west, and in between there's near-desert, rolling hills, wild country, and just about everything else." He considered. "Except cities." Cities with big theaters.

"What's the land like around Knighton and on your ranch?"

"Runs from a bit of broken flats up into the foothills of the Big Horn Mountains. We're on the eastern slope of the Big Horns."

"Mountains?" She sounded intrigued.

"Big Horns aren't the Rockies," he said, so she wouldn't have a mistaken image. "They're older mountains, so they've been worn down. Look rounder, sort of. Though they've got their ways, too."

"What's that mean?"

"Means they'll catch you out if you get cocky. Bring you down if don't give them the respect they deserve. Flip side, they provide good water from the snow melt, so it's greener than a lot of the state. That's why my dad's grandfather settled there. Each generation's added to his parcel, bit by bit. Starting from longhorns from Texas in the 1870s, we've kept making the stock better. What's that look for?"

"You love it."

"I love it."

She nodded slowly. "Why?"

They walked a minute, maybe more while he considered. When he spoke it wasn't anything he'd known he'd say. "Ranching and Wyoming do something I've never heard of anything else doing. They make you small and they make you big all at the same time. You watch a calf being born and know you're no more than an attendant on Nature's parade, sweeping up after the elephants."

He heard her warm chuckle, and appreciated it.

"But then you have a heifer that's stuck so good she'll never get out of a fence tangle, and if you weren't there, right then, fighting her and the fence and rain pouring down and clippers not working worth a damn, you know—you *know*—she'd have died. There you were. Not ten years old, and you did it, and you felt so big your head should poke a hole in the thunderclouds overhead.

"The Slash-C … I can breathe there. Breathe in deep and slow, and know I've filled my lungs with something good. It can be a harsh land, but it doesn't play favorites. And there's a beauty … I can't tell you, not right. I'm not good with words."

"You're doing just fine."

He met her gaze. And stopped right there outside the stock show, surrounded by people and animals milling around with the busyness of departure, and kissed this woman whose amazing hazel eyes went soft with reflecting his emotions back to him.

The kiss left them both breathless. It might have done a lot more if a wolf whistle and some chuckles hadn't penetrated her consciousness.

They stood there, looking at each other for a dozen breaths.

What is happening here?

Lust. It had to be. A potent enough case of lust that she was going to make love with this man tonight. No matter what. And despite the fact that she knew—*knew*—there was no future, because his ship was headed back to Knighton, and hers was aimed for whatever stop came next on the way to Broadway.

At last, Ed sucked in a final deep breath, held the exhibition hall's big door, then took her hand and led her in.

She was Alice through the looking glass. Stepping into a world she had never known before. Never considered before.

And he was her guide.

They wandered hand in hand. Some would not view the emptying space as a romantic venue, considering the need to sidestep certain hazards from cattle, as well as the odor impossible to sidestep. But this was his world, and she saw he moved through it with a confidence that also included humility, bringing it a grace that made her heart lift and hammer.

"Ed, glad to see you." A lanky man with a lush mustache extended his hand. "Missed you yesterday. I'd hoped to have a word."

"Mr. Gates, good to see you, too. This is—" He smiled down at her. "—Donna Roberts. Donna, this is Mr. Gates, one of the best cattlemen in this country."

A smile spread under the mustache. "If you're going to say things like that, you'd both best call me Carter. Miss," he added, lifting the front of his hat. "Can't talk long. Need to find that scamp of mine and get started back. Tucker's probably driving some poor soul to distraction with his questions."

"They're good questions," Ed said. "I was part of a group hanging around for the answers to his questions to those folks from Texas showing the paint horses."

Pride showed in the older man's eyes, but he shook his head. "I'll be lucky if he's not headed south with them, everything forgotten but wanting to know more. But what I want to talk to you about if your young lady here doesn't mind is more on your thoughts about crossbreeding continentals with Herefords."

"I don't mind at all," Donna said. Not when she saw how the older man's interest lit Ed's eyes.

She listened carefully, and understood about every third word.

But while she didn't understand much of the spoken language, their body language didn't require translation.

Ed was respectful toward the older man, yet sure in what he was saying.

For his part, Carter Gates started interested, and ended deeply impressed. Donna fought back a temptation to beam at him when he expressed the sentiment.

"You coming to the National Western?" Carter Gates asked.

"Afraid not."

"That's a shame. They've opened to crossbreeds, and others would be interested in what you're doing. If you decide to bring stock down, you let me know, and we'll find you a spot with ours in the barns."

"I appreciate that, Carter."

They parted, but as she and Ed continued walking past display areas being dismantled and animals being led out, she quickly realized Carter Gates was not alone in being interested in and impressed by what Ed was doing on the Slash-C.

She flashed back to watching him at the opening night party, talking to those heavyhitters. She would have been jittery and overly talkative. But Ed was at ease with others, because he was at ease with himself.

Because he knew who he was and what he wanted to do.

But … she knew who she was and what she wanted to do, too.

She did.

"And they talk about theater being a small world," she said as the rancher said farewell. "You must know every soul here."

It had gone on like that all morning, through their lunch at a food stand, and now the afternoon.

"Cattle can be a fairly small world, but what we're doing here is new, and that's an even smaller world. At the National Western, I'd be a speck in the ocean."

"That's the big show in January? You mentioned that, then we got sidetracked by rodeo."

"Rodeo and other things." His grin was as potent as the first kiss his words recalled. Memory of the sensations of that kiss, her responses, and all that had followed sparked through her.

"Can't you get away other times of the year?" Her voice sounded breathless and throaty, at odds with the prosaic question.

"Spring's calving season, planting, and repairing what winter brought down. Summer's caring for stock and doing your best sunup to sundown to keep up. Then you're into roundup and weaning and getting 'em ready for market. Winter's your most downtime. So that's when ranchers go to stock shows."

She'd had little to do with farms growing up in Indianapolis, but being surrounded by some of the most fertile cropland in the world made it impossible for even a self-absorbed theater-mad teenager not to know farmers didn't have anything like the 40-hour work-week and annual vacation package of the suburbs. A year-round and lifelong commitment.

Like marriage.

"Oh, look at the size of those." She pointed rather wildly at animals in a parallel aisle.

He looked around. "European stock. Most American cattle, like the Herefords, Angus you're probably familiar with, give good meat production. If we can breed bigger European seedstock in while keeping meat quality, we'll have the best of both."

"Seedstock?"

"That's what I came to see. Animals available for breeding into our herd. It's fine to research the lines, but watching the animals move, getting an idea of temperament, that's important, too."

"You're a trailblazer in this, aren't you?"

He lifted a shoulder. "I'm doing some."

"What does your mom think? And your father?"

"Dad can tell a bull from a heifer without help, but the law is what he cares about. Mom? She'd have us going full-bore. In fact, she did that with a small subherd. Trouble is, the meat's not as good as we want for Slash-C brand. I'm taking it cautious with the main herd. Being real careful what lines we breed in."

She understood the gist, while glimpsing the complexities and variables behind his explanation. Like theater, there was another universe backstage. "You should do it," she said.

"What?"

"Come back to the big show in January."

He shook his head. "Not this year. Maybe never."

"But, Ed, all these people have said it would be a great opportunity for you."

Each one had urged him to bring some of his livestock. She'd also heard the show included rodeo events, a horse show, singing, dances, and parties. She ignored twinges at images of him singing, dancing, and partying without her. It wasn't like she expected him never to sing, dance, party … or love … after this week.

"It's hard on everyone when I'm gone, even in winter. It leaves Mom and a couple of hands who were old when she was born." He shook his head again.

Yet he'd stayed on. For her.

After an early dinner at a place one of Ed's friends recommended— she had never seen steaks that big—they returned to the hotel.

The transformation of its lobby shoved aside her rising nerves.

Christmas had arrived at staid Rockton Hotel.

Sort of.

A tree stood in the lobby, with smaller tree-like decorations spotted around, including at either end of the front desk, squeezing the clerks.

"It's pink," Ed said, in apparent disbelief. "Pink and fuzzy."

Pink, fuzzy, and sporting aqua balls and an encircling magenta streamer.

"I think it's supposed to look like it's been flocked," she said. "Unless—Oh, God, I hope they didn't do that to a real tree. It's got to be a fake tree. It's got to be…"

They stood side by side in front of it, staring. He took her hand in his, and she leaned her shoulder against his arm.

"So your tree won't look like this?" he asked.

"I won't have one this year. Not unless my parents can find one when I have a break in January. You?"

"Won't look anything like this. Live tree, decorations mixed from several generations, and what my sister and I made as kids."

She smiled at the thought of his parents bringing out his creations each year.

"Everybody together, piling into the car for the tree lot, looking for the right one," she said. "Balsam for that wonderful scent."

He caught on right away. "All together, yeah, but on horseback, finding a fir from the mountains. Smells like outdoors."

"Multicolored lights. Not the tiny ones."

"Right."

"Tinsel," she said.

"Garland."

"No flocking," they said in unison, and laughed.

"Star on top," she said.

"Angel. Looks a lot like you, actually."

She looked into his eyes, and felt that spotlight sensation of their first meeting multiplied a hundred times…. Except now she realized it was also the feeling from the opening night party of a line connecting them. Together, those feelings had informed her precisely where he sat whenever he was in the audience.

His smile faded. "What's wrong, Donna?"

"Nothing's wrong. Absolutely nothing." She sucked in a breath. "It's time for us to go to your room now."

Heat flared into his eyes first. Heat that burned into her lungs and all the way down to the pit of her stomach. Oh, yes, he wanted her. Let him even try to say he didn't.

"Donna—"

"Forget it, Ed. Most times that quiet sternness might do the trick. Not this time. Your room. Now." She started for the elevator.

CHAPTER TEN

Monday night

He hadn't been able to argue in the elevator because a businessman stepped in with them at the last second.

Good.

When they reached Ed's floor, she marched down the hallway ahead, stopping by his door.

"Donna?"

"Open the door unless you want me to do something scandalous right here in the hall," she threatened.

She had to do it this way. Before she ran out of courage.

Because she knew she'd run out of courage long before she ran out of wanting, a recipe for going stark-raving mad. After the past three nights, alone in her bed, she knew that for sure.

He unlocked the door, letting her enter an even smaller version of the room she shared with Lydia.

As soon as the door clicked closed, she turned and faced him.

"I was going to seduce you Friday night—"

"*Friday?*"

"—but you insisted on riding back in the bus. Yes, Friday. Why'd you say it like that?"

"I thought you were trying Saturday night—"

"I was. *And* last night."

His grin appeared at her mournful tone. "You were so tired. And you weren't sure." He cupped her shoulders, studying her. "You're not sure now."

"I am sure."

Despite herself, her eyes flickered to the bed. The bed was narrow. He was a big man. Tall, broad … and long.

"If you don't—I'm not, I mean I don't—But you have no way of knowing that, and if you don't want someone so forward—"

He took her face in his big hands. "I know."

She tipped her head back, preparing to ask what he thought he knew, maybe even hoping she'd ease her nerves by teasing him. At his expression her breath caught sharp, pulling back her words, along with the scent of his skin, and a knowledge so powerful that it stung fast, undeniable tears into her eyes.

His eyes were hot with desire, a fire that raced through her blood, too. But she'd seen men's eyes hot with desire. She'd even reciprocated the feeling.

It had never brought tears.

Ed's eyes, though, also held a warmth so deep and so enduring she thought she could never get to the end of it.

That brought her tears.

He raised one big hand, cupping the back of her head, and drawing her wet face against his shoulder.

"I know."

He held her while she cried, letting warmth enfold her, holding off the heat for this moment.

She sniffled against his shirt.

"Are all the men in Wyoming like you?"

"They would try to be if they met you."

He'd lifted her into his arms then, carried her to the bed, and held her so very gently.

And they'd fallen asleep.

They fell asleep.

She had to be the least seductive seductress in the universe.

Donna had blinked awake a moment ago, torn between wanting to stay in exactly this position—spooned against him with his arms wrapped around her—for as long as her heart beat, and wanting to leap out of bed and disappear.

They hadn't even gotten their clothes off. Their shoes and socks, yes, but otherwise a full complement of inside clothes.

Which was a shame.

Because if she didn't have on blouse and bra, all she'd have to do would be to slide her arm a little and his hand would be on her breast, his fingers in just the right spot to touch her nipple, which was doing its part to make the connection.

Though why he would want to bother with someone who fell asleep for heaven's sake—

"You're awake?" His low-voiced words stirred her hair.

"Yes. I'm sorry. I—"

"No need to be sorry. You needed to sleep." He ran his palm up and down her arm. "You work hard."

"I'm not sleepy now." She aimed for sultry. It came out Ado Annie. Dammit.

She took hold of his hand and put it over her breast. Made a *mmm* sound, though she didn't feel much except the weight of his touch. Then she set to unbuttoning her blouse.

She was doing this. She was really doing this. She wanted to. She wanted him … She did.

"Donna, honey, we don't have to—"

"I want to. I really want to." Her hands stilled. They hadn't made much progress anyway for the shaking. "Unless you don't—"

"It's pretty clear I do." He pressed tighter against her derriere, and she knew that to be fact.

"Good, then we'll get rid of these clothes."

She sat up, partially turning toward him as she pulled the shirt over her head, shook out her hair, gave him what she hoped was an alluring smile … and slid off the side of the bed.

CHAPTER ELEVEN

Monday night

"Donna! Are you okay?"

"Other than my pride, I'm fine." But she didn't lift her head. She sat against the side of the bed, knees drawn up, head down, so her hair curtained her face.

He adjusted so he could get up without having his own pride issues, and moved around the bed. He sat to stroke his hand over that silken hair, down to the nape of her neck, let it rest there.

When she still didn't look up, he went for more direct action.

He stood, stripped his jeans and socks, then started on his shirt.

Apparently feeling the flutter of fabric as he let the shirt go, she turned her head, still cradled in her arms. When his t-shirt followed, she finally looked up.

He bent and picked her up, carrying her high to avoid contact with the part of him clamoring for total contact *now*.

"Wha—What are you doing?"

"Taking you to bed."

"Ed."

He stopped, still holding her. "If you say no, we won't."

Apparently addressing his chest, she said, "I'm not saying no."

"I could use more enthusiasm." *Like hell. If he were any more enthusiastic, this would be over before they started.*

"Yes." It was a bit subdued, but not uncertain. Then she put her mouth over his skin and sucked lightly.

Exultation surged through him, dampened only by the need to

corral his … *enthusiasm.*

He hitched her to one arm, pulling down the covers, then placed her carefully on the bed.

Before he considered what next, she unzipped her jeans, bent her knees, lifted her rump, and shucked jeans and underpants off in one, fluid motion that made his knees go weak.

Then she pulled the sheet over herself in instinctive caution, all the way over the bra she still wore and up to her chin.

To give her time and to put himself on the line first, he removed his briefs.

Her eyes widened in a way that made him swell even more, at the same time he dredged up every bit of restraint he had to put on a condom taken from the nightstand drawer.

Making no effort to dislodge the end of the sheet she clutched by her chin, he pulled it loose from the bottom, leaving it covering her from mid-thigh up. God, her legs were beautiful. Dancer strong and curved and smooth.

He stroked the one closer to him, but only once. He couldn't take more.

He started to join her on the bed.

That's when things began to slide out of his control.

Under the sheet, she shifted as he lowered himself to the bed … and he nestled directly into the cradle between her legs.

He closed his eyes, and swore to himself. He'd intended to put his legs outside hers, to delay this contact, just a little.

She squirmed, the sheet slid away from between them, and that was nearly the end of it right there. He breathed, slow and deliberate. Grasping for something else, anything else.

She still wore her bra. He shifted to the side slightly to free one arm, careful not to get too near the bed's edge. He stroked the soft, sweet rise above the cup of her plain bra, toying with the fabric to let his finger slide under.

She reached back, unhooked the bra, and tossed it away. So much for that delay.

He kissed down the elegant curve of her breast, absorbing the softness with tongue and lips. Then the beaded, rounded tip that came into his mouth so perfectly. He drew on it, flicked it with his tongue, then drew again.

She arched her back, drawing him deeper into the cradle of her legs, and he rocked with her. She moaned, a sound felt through every part of him that touched her, that covered her, that sought entrance to her.

He couldn't wait any longer. Couldn't.

He positioned himself and slid in.

Sucking and rocking.

Harder and faster. This wasn't going to last. It wasn't going to be long enough.

He felt her straining to get the rhythm.

He was an idiot.

"Relax," he said, trying to keep torment out of his voice.

She raised her hips, hard, and fast, just as he shifted slower.

He slid out, then returned, barely inside her. Muscles taut with the effort of not driving into her.

She made a sound of frustration.

"Slow. We have time."

"I *want* you," she said. What man wouldn't want to hear that, then multiply it by a couple billion because she said it to him. But then subtract a few because it came through gritted teeth.

"You have me."

Her eyes flew open.

"You have me," he repeated. And stroked into her, deep and deeper. Slow. Agonizingly slow. Allowing himself what he craved only in a time measured in eons.

She gasped, gasped again with the second, slow deep thrust, then another. He would die in this slowness. He would die, and that was okay. He stroked again, sweat slicking his limbs, his muscles and nerves and tendons tortured by slowness. And again.

Until she pulsed around him with short gusts of breath that held music in them, because they were hers.

His release came then, hard, held back it seemed forever, sur-rounded by that music of her.

She wrapped her arms around his shoulders as he dropped onto her, and he felt her sigh across his face.

It was a beginning.

He rolled off her, but at the same time, slid his arm under her neck, curling her toward him, so her head rested against his shoulder.

That was the most in sync they'd been.

She knew rhythm, and they hadn't had it.

She tugged the sheet up, even though it didn't separate them at all, and only covered one of her breasts and a shoulder.

He gave a *Mmmm* of … what? *Satisfaction?* Well, she supposed, technically, they had both been satisfied.

But…

Maybe she'd built it up too much. Gearing herself to seduce him four nights in row. Maybe that made it natural to feel some … awkwardness?

He made the sound again and she tipped her head to see his face.

"Why are you smiling?" She felt both surprise and suspicion.

His mouth stretched into the grin she loved. Her nipples tightened, one under the sheet and the other pressed against his chest, apparently feeling no suspicion at all.

"Because we got past the first time." He opened his eyes, shifting so her head rested on the pillow while he propped himself on an elbow over her, his eyes burning with heat. "And now we get to start the practice that makes for perfect."

He took her mouth, his tongue plunging in, at the same time he slid a finger inside of her, with his thumb brushing across her nub. Her back arched off the bed as she came hard, just that fast, gasping out his name.

They'd determined they were both hungry. But with no all-night room service at the Rockton Hotel, and absolutely no possibility they were getting out of this bed, they shared a candy bar he'd had in his bag, and two miniature packets of peanuts from her purse.

His stomach rumbled. She patted its flat surface and instructed, "Pretend you're having turkey for Christmas dinner."

"Beef."

"Unh-unh. Has to be turkey. And stuffing."

"Scalloped potatoes."

"Asparagus."

He clicked his tongue in disapproval. "No sense filling up on vegetables with dessert still to come."

"Cookies."

"Pie, pie, and more pie."

"That's Thanksgiving," she protested.

"Then, too. Pie. Also for my birthday."

"You have a birthday *pie?*"

"No, I have birthday pies."

She opened her mouth, then closed it. "What kind of pie?"

"Every kind I can get."

"But what's your favorite?"

"My grandmother's apple pie." His eyes closed in bliss. "There is nothing better."

She bit her lip. She baked cookies, but she'd only made pie a couple times. Could she—not that it mattered. She wasn't going to be making him pie.

"What?" he demanded.

"What what?" She blinked fast.

"Why'd you get all misty on me?"

"Christmas, I guess."

"Huh. I thought maybe you felt the same way I do about pie."

She swatted his muscled abdomen. He caught her hand to slide it over his ribs, then lower. Pie was forgotten.

Ed Currick definitely believed in practice. Lots and lots of practice. His approach took all the pressure off.

Even when they'd both fallen out of bed. That time, he'd calmly scooped her up, placed her gently on the bed, then shoved it against the wall so they only had one side to worry about.

Then he'd gotten back into bed as if nothing had happened. All part of the process.

They were practicing, learning each other's bodies. Nothing was a mistake, nothing was awkward. It was all learning. All practice.

No need to expect fireworks. If they came, fine…

And they did. Her. Him. And the fireworks. They all came. And came again. *Oh, my.*

She found enough energy to raise her head from where she was wedged between his big body and the wall, and watched him as he slept.

She'd first seen him Wednesday. Had first talked to him Thursday. Had first kissed him that same night. Had first made love with him Monday.

Never had she fallen so precipitously into a relationship. Days? Her usual style was months. Sometimes years.

If she had it to do over again, she would climb over that pile of luggage and right into his arms.

He woke from a dream that felt nothing like a dream.

He'd been on the Slash-C. Riding. Mid-summer. He knew that with utter certainty from the look and smell and *feel* of everything around him.

The light was a particular clarity that came to his home, just before the sun dropped behind the Big Horns. As if the last beams of the day held enough brightness to imprint each mental snapshot through the longest, darkest night.

He was in the foothills, in a spot he knew so well he could plot out each rock, bush, and gully. It afforded a sweeping view across his family's land.

The land he belonged to. The land had filled him, as he'd told her, making him bigger and smaller at the same time. Making him who he was. It felt entirely right.

Then he'd seen, unexpected, a mass of snowberries.

Their bright white berries caught his eye. They'd looked so perfect, so right.

Only now, awake, did he recognize the dream's flaw.

He'd never seen snowberries there before. Ever.

It was a southern slope at a lower elevation, home to tough native grasses and sage that could take the dry. Snowberry needed a lot more moisture to grow anywhere near that low, so it would be only on a northern slope. Never a southern slope. Not there. Made no sense.

And the wrong season completely for the berries. Spring they bloomed, summer the shrubs held their green leafs. Fall into winter, that's when the clusters of white berries came.

In the heat of summer? No.

Dreams made things like that happen—snowberries with dazzling white berries in the heat of summer—but that wasn't real.

The Slash-C was real. That was his life. That was *him*.

But that wasn't what she wanted.

He stroked her hair from her cheek, so softly he was sure it wouldn't wake her. It didn't. Yet she turned into his touch, making a low, soft sound.

But he was what she wanted.

Heat surged through him with memories of her body, opening and welcoming him, until he had to shift with the swelling.

But, no, it wasn't only physical.

The words hadn't been spoken between them—maybe neither of them wanted the importance of those words to hone the knife that would soon cut them apart. But he recognized her feelings for him in her touches, in her need for him.

If he cared for her less maybe he'd even use that against her, to try to get her to give this up, to come to Wyoming with him.

Except he couldn't imagine caring for her less. Only caring for her more and more. He already knew the one thing he could give her was to never ask her to give up what she wanted for him.

He closed his eyes and hoped he wouldn't dream again.

Because it had been all wrong, his dream. No matter how beautiful the snowberries had looked, no matter how he had felt seeing them there. Snowberries didn't grow as his dream had imagined.

The wrong place, the wrong season.

He gathered her to him, and held her.

CHAPTER TWELVE

Tuesday

Donna's hand stopped mid-swipe across the fogged bathroom mirror. Their efforts to work around the disparity in their heights to make love in the shower had filled the room with steam, even after Ed's exit let billows escape.

It was her reflection that stopped her.

Her eyes looked tired. Like someone short on sleep. Her mouth was puffy. There were pink patches on her throat and jaw from Ed's stubble. Lower, too.

She had never looked better.

They'd finally gotten up for something to eat around noon. Then they'd returned to the room, and bed. Only with the winter afternoon waning to evening had she accepted the need to prepare for tonight's performance.

The real world of make believe was about to intrude on the make believe reality of these past hours.

Try to intrude.

They had only these few days. With such a short time, surely they could sustain the sense that nothing existed beyond the two of them. Like the bubble they'd been in at the Mexican restaurant.

Their bubble would stretch enough for her to do what she needed to do. She could stay inside it even onstage, because she'd feel him out there in the audience. The two of them in their bubble, no matter what existed outside.

Until the very last moment.

"I have something I want you to see," Ed said when she came out of the bathroom.

"I should be getting to the theater. If I miss final call, Brad will burst."

"I'll get you there on time."

He sounded solemn. That worried her a little. Yet she knew he *would* get her to the theater on time.

"Okay."

"Good."

A short, simple word, quickly lost amid putting on outdoor clothes and making sure she had her bag for the theater. Yet she felt his deep pleasure at her acceptance.

Their taxi pulled up to the curb.

Donna was surprised Ed had a taxi waiting outside the hotel. Even more surprised at where it dropped them off. There were large buildings at either end, with nothing but space here in the middle. Like a football field set down among government buildings.

"Here?" she asked, though Ed was already telling the driver to pick them up at this spot in 20 minutes.

"Here," he confirmed. He came around the taxi and opened the door, drawing her to her feet.

"Why?"

"Be patient. C'mon, let's go."

Still holding her hand, he led her to the center of the open space. On a football field, this is where the captains would meet for the coin toss. A spattering of pedestrians passed.

"That," he said, turning her to face one direction, "is the State Capitol. Not as impressive as Wyoming's, but then I'm biased."

"It's very nice, but I don't understand—"

"Now, let's head west." He turned her 180 degrees to start down an arrow-straight pathway.

"What's that?" she asked, pointing ahead.

"That's west. If it were daylight and clear you'd see the Rockies."

"I meant that building, the big one with curved wings like arms reaching out."

"We'll get to that. First, over to your right's the seal pond, with statues of seals, though the fountains aren't on this time of year. The curved colonnade around it is a memorial to a guy named Voorhies, apparently because he paid for it. Past that and set forward more is Denver's original library—one of Andrew Carnegie's libraries. But a while back, the city built a new library."

"How do you know all this?"

"I studied up to be your tour guide. You said you felt bad you haven't seen much of Denver."

She had said that, hadn't she? Her priorities had shifted, but that didn't make it any less sweet that he'd done this for her.

At a point where the path demanded a left or right turn, he stopped. Wind skidded around them. She tucked her arm into his and huddled closer. He disengaged his arm, but only to put it around her, so she had no complaints.

"Over that way, is the Greek Theater—an outdoor amphitheater. You should be able to see some of the main library—no, straight. Now, look between the Greek Theater's columns. That's the new art museum."

"This is amazing. You are amazing." She turned, reaching to put her arms around his neck. "I don't know what to say."

"What I'd say—well, I *should* sing it, since it's one those Fred Astaire songs Grover told me about, but I'm no singer. I'm thinking of one called 'They Can't Take That Away From Me.' "

She knew it, knew every line. It was a man storing up every memory he could before the separation he knew was coming. She swallowed against a knot in her throat.

Ed said, "There's a line that says she's changed his lif—"

She stopped him with her thumb crossing his lips, her gloved hand to his cheek. If he reached the lyric about the lovers never meeting again, she'd dissolve.

He kissed her thumb, then straightened, put his hands to her shoulders, and turned her to face the view.

"Okay. No time. We have more landmarks to point out. Now we get to the building straight ahead. This is the Denver City and County Building." She giggled at his exaggerated tour guide manner, and in appreciation of his breaking the mood. He checked his watch. "A handsome bit of architecture, the municipal center of the city, and any second…"

Light exploded in front of her. She gasped. First with surprise, then, a second time, with pleasure.

What had simply been a mass of a building sparkled in drenching color.

"Oh, Christmas lights! All the way to the top of the tower."

"Clock tower," he said, and she heard the grin in his voice. "One-hundred and eighty-feet tall."

"Oh, Ed." She turned from the glorious lights to him, wonder welling inside her. Wonder at what she'd seen. Wonder at his giving it to her. Wonder at him. "Oh, Ed."

She stretched up, but couldn't have kissed him if he hadn't cooperated … which he did.

He partially straightened. With her arms around his neck, she came off the ground, holding on, kissing him.

"Damn," he said against her mouth.

"Wha—"

"Time," he said. "Theater."

"Oh," she acknowledged dazedly. Right. The theater. Tonight's performance.

He scooped her up, which suited her fine, since it brought their faces closer. Though kissing became more difficult as he strode back the way they'd come. She settled for kissing his cheek, his jaw, his neck. He growled. So she did it again.

She was aware of being bundled into the taxi, of the driver chuckling and saying something about Ed carrying her. Then Ed was beside her, his arms back around her, and … ah … his mouth on hers.

Too soon, far too soon, he pulled back and said, "We're here."

Nearly. Oh, yes, very nearly.

He kissed her one last time. "You've got to go. You'll be late."

"Aren't you—" No, of course he wasn't coming with her. She had to go on stage. He would be in the audience.

She started away, trying to force herself to hurry.

"Young man, I've never told a fare this before, but you've overpaid," she heard the taxi driver say, laughter in his voice.

"No, sir," Ed said. "Because I'm going to need to sit here a bit before I can go anywhere."

Donna bit her lip to hold back a giggle, along with a temptation a whole lot hotter, and broke into a run for the stage door.

CHAPTER THIRTEEN

Tuesday Night

"Great show, Donna."

She turned from her spot at the end of the communal dressing room and saw Stan Henson's head poked around the door frame. The director didn't travel with the company, but he and others arrived periodically to catch performances and fine-tune.

"Come see me after you change," he ordered.

She thought of Ed waiting. But you didn't say "Catch you later, I have a date" to the director.

She dressed fast, then had trouble finding the man, who seemed to cover every square inch of backstage. Always a minute ahead of her. She heard "He just left" a dozen times.

She rushed into wardrobe, and ran smack into him. If she'd been bigger she would have knocked him over. Instead, he took two steps back, regained his balance and laughed. "Gotta love your enthusiasm, Donna. C'mon, let's go to the offices."

She wanted to tell him to spit out whatever he had to say here because she didn't want to waste time going up, only to have to backtrack to find Ed. But the director was already heading away, and arguing would take more time.

She fidgeted in the chair he'd gestured her to while he went out and called to someone named Marty. Finally—*finally*—he came and sat behind the desk.

"I'll make this fast—"

Not fast enough.

"—I've been watching you. Tonight was your best dancing."

She barely stopped her jaw from dropping. She'd been sore enough—and distracted by memories of how she'd gotten sore—that she'd hardly thought about her dancing.

"Your singing's top-notch. Strong enough that you carry some of the others. Your acting's held you back. I told you that in New York. But you've improved. Thought you had promise on my last visit, but tonight I saw more. A glow. A joy. Wasn't there before, but you had it in spades tonight. I won't give you the run-around—"

Even if he had, her head couldn't spin any faster than it was now.

"—we're expecting a cast change, and we want to move you into Nikki—"

A speaking role. Then, "Lydia."

He made a *tching* sound. One did not question Stan Henson's proclamations, even if they struck down a friend. But her stomach had been roiling from the beginning of this conversation, and it must have been from a premonition about Lydia. Had to be.

"You'll keep this under your hat. Nora's leaving stop after next." An added mumble sounded like *Not soon enough.* "That will give you a chance to rehearse—you as Nikki and Lydia as Helene—so you're comfortable before San Francisco." He leaned forward, sharp eyes examining her. "But it's you I want you thinking about. If you handle this the way I think you will, it could be just the start."

She gaped at him.

"You'll stay as Charity understudy. Not that we expect Angela to go anywhere."

His certainty indicated Angela had not gotten the TV job Maudie had mentioned, whether their lead knew it or not.

Donna mumbled words of pleasure, excitement, and thanks. He clucked his amusement, discomfort, and understanding.

But he didn't understand, she thought, as she rushed back through the theater. He couldn't possibly. Because she didn't.

She pushed open the stage door, saw Ed and launched herself at him, he caught her, wrapping his arms securely around her, and she didn't let go for a long time.

They had now.

They would have these days where reality floated past outside their bubble.

They had to have that.

She told Ed about the director's news as they started walking, her hand warm and protected within his.

"That's terrific, Donna. It's a big step, and you'll keep on making those steps."

She'd always planned to. "First, I have to do okay with Nikki."

"You will. You'll be fantastic in this role and beyond."

He believed that—Ed wouldn't lie to her. And *she* believed she would be fantastic. So why wasn't she as excited as she would have expected to be?

"Wish I could see you in the new role." Something jolted through her, but before she grabbed hold of it, he gave her a shrewd look, then drew in a breath, and said, "Smells like snow. So, what's your favorite Christmas smell?"

She recognized and welcomed the distraction he offered. "The tree. You?"

"Pies baking."

"I should have guessed. I also love cookies just out of the oven."

"Pies baking."

"The turkey."

"Pies baking. Favorite flavor, too."

"Cinnamon."

"Pies—"

"I know. Pies baking."

"Actually, I was going to say: Pies done baking. God, I'm hungry."

She laughed. "Aren't you always?"

He looked at her, and heat pulsed through her. "Yeah, I am. Always. How about takeout? Grover told me about a Chinese place around the corner from the hotel."

"Takeout?" She immediately saw the advantage. But she wanted him to say it.

His voice dropped. "We could take it back to the room."

"Oh?"

"Or we could eat there," he amended, almost masking the disappointment. "Or find another restaurant. If you don't like Chinese—"

"I love Chinese. And takeout would be—" Their gazes caught, held. "—great."

He tucked her against his side as they moved down the sidewalk hip to hip.

"But, Ed," she said after half a block. "I won't be able to breathe if we keep up this pace."

"Sorry. I didn't realize—Guess I forgot." As the pace slowed from supersonic to merely breakneck, he said, "I was telling Grover about the Christmas lights. He said he might take Maudie to see them."

She smiled at his effort to give their thoughts another path.

"There's a legend that outdoor lights started here in Denver in 1914. A boy was so sick he had to stay in bed, so his electrician father dipped bulbs in red and green and strung them up in a tree he could see from his room. A few years later the father was a consultant when the city started—"

"What happened to the boy?"

He looked over at her. "I have no idea."

She *humphed* in dissatisfaction.

"But I can tell you that most years the lights come on at six each night from after Thanksgiving to the New Year, then back on for the Western National Stock Show in January."

"But you're not coming back for that, right?" She heard the off note in her voice, and from the look he shot her, so did he.

She had to face it. She didn't like the idea of his being here without her. And that was horrible. She should encourage him the way he'd encouraged her about getting the role of Nikki.

"Maybe another year, if we have a few good years in a row."

"You will," she said with certainty. But her mind was on that other track: Was she less excited about the new role than she would have expected because he wouldn't see her in it?

"Here's the restaurant," Ed said.

She heard strain in his voice. Knew it was from impatience, because she felt that, too. She gladly concentrated on that instead of her thoughts.

"I hope they're fast." As she ducked under the arm he extended to hold the door she slanted a look at him.

"Can't be fast enough," he muttered.

They ate the food cold, and then a second round of it even colder. Because they had better things to do.

With the two of them nestled in the bed, she unwrapped a cookie and broke it in half.

"What's the fortune say?"

She dropped the paper onto the night stand. "I don't want to know. They're bossy things, those fortunes."

"Just thought I should be prepared if it says something like, 'You'll die in bed soon, a happy man.' "

She giggled and held out half the cookie to him.

He raised his head to snag the cookie from her fingers, then kept coming, his mouth open on the flesh where her shoulder met her collarbone.

She closed her eyes, absorbing sensations.

"Your skin is so white, so smooth. Like…"

When he went silent, she prodded, "Like?"

"Snowberries."

"What?"

But he didn't answer. He bent his head, and slid his tongue along the slope of her breast, then over its tip, sending a jolt through her that clenched her inner muscles.

"Snowberries?" She had to pause to pant in two quick breaths.

"Those are the ones with the white——?"

He raised his head, leaving her skin moist and warm, and wanting more. "Berries."

He lifted her hand, and directed the forgotten cookie half she still held to her lips. She took it in her mouth with a flick of her tongue.

He groaned. "I take it back."

"What?" she murmured.

"My favorite Christmas flavor. I have a new one."

"I don't believe it. Something better than pie?"

"Um-hum. You."

CHAPTER FOURTEEN

Wednesday

When they woke to Wednesday's daylight, he asked, "Want to tour Denver?"

"Yesterday was wonderful, but no." She wanted to stay here. With him. In their bubble.

As long as they could.

"Okay." After a pause, he added, "You know, I've been thinking about that shower. I've got an idea…"

"I'm all for ideas."

Especially ones that worked so well. So very, very well.

"Good performance tonight, Donna. Not sure how many in the audience saw it, though. You ever going to do something about Angela?"

Brad had blocked her exit by stepping in front of her in the narrow corridor.

He didn't seem to need an answer to his question, snorting out a breath, and saying, "Your guy's down by the door, has his head together with that doorkeeper." Then he moved on.

She found Ed still with Grover.

"What were you two talking about?" she asked Ed as they headed out.

"Did you know he used to dance on TV? Variety shows."

"Really?"

"Yup. Know who he—what do they call it—backed up? Fred Astaire."

She stopped. "Really? No. He was probably telling you a story."

"I don't think so. Maudie believes him."

"Oh, my gosh. Oh, my *gosh.*"

"Yeah, I thought you'd be interested. So, here's what I thought we'd do—go get sandwiches from the diner, and take them back to the theater, including some for Grover, and you can ask him questions to your heart's content."

She hesitated, part of her wanting to hurry back to the hotel, to have the time to themselves. But he looked so pleased with himself ... "You think he'd be okay with that?"

"I know he'd be okay with that, as long as I get his sandwich order right."

"Thank you, Ed. Thank you. That would be wonderful. I can't imagine sitting around a cold theater eating sandwiches and listening to old show biz stories is your idea of fun."

"It'll be fun watching you have fun. As long as—" He looked at her with such intensity that heat flowed through her body in immediate response. "—it doesn't go real late."

"Not late. Not late at all."

He smiled. "Besides, Grover gave me the chance to find out Henri was exactly right about that song 'I Won't Dance'—it definitely was about *not* dancing."

CHAPTER FIFTEEN

Thursday

The dazed peace that enveloped Donna each time they made love had started to slip away.

At least the dazed part. The peace remained.

She was on her side, pressed against Ed, as he lay on his back. Her cheek on his chest, his arm around her, her leg over his, his hand lightly rubbing her back.

He rolled his head toward the window. "Snowing," he observed. "Looks like it'll stick."

"Mmm." If it snowed enough would they close the theater? That would be an unexpected gift. The one she most wanted now.

All I want for Christmas is...

No, better not to think about that.

"Open presents Christmas morning," she said.

He picked up her lead. "Christmas Eve. Gotta care for the animals Christmas morning."

"Christmas Eve's for going to church."

"Do that after tending the animals on Christmas Day."

"Also need Christmas Eve to finish wrapping. Picking out the right paper for the person getting the gift, finding a different combination of paper and ribbon for each package, making the bows."

"Wrap it simple. A box with a ribbon. Only Mom does bows."

"Everybody hangs a Christmas stocking."

"Really? Adults, too?"

"Oh, yes."

"Hmm. I think we might have to adopt that one."

"Of course it means you buy things to fill the other stockings."

"Maybe not, then."

She swatted his chest lightly. "Selfish!"

"Hey, it's hard enough trying to figure out something to get my mother for a present."

"What about your Dad?"

"That's no problem. He's a man."

They entwined the fingers of their right hands. If he hadn't bent his elbow, she wouldn't have been able to reach. But he did, bringing their hands together atop his chest.

"You don't talk much about your father, not as much as you do about your mother."

"Huh. Maybe because Mom and I work together on the ranch. Dad's a lawyer in town."

"He doesn't live with you on the ranch?"

He looked surprised. "Of course he does. It's his family's ranch. He inherited half, then he and Mom bought out Uncle Gordon when he moved to California. But Dad goes into town to his office most days. Though anybody with a problem's likely to come by the ranch for help, too. He helped a guy a few years back who didn't have money, but did have a real nice bull. Breeding in that bloodline's done a lot for our herd. Mom keeps asking Dad to find more clients with good breeding stock."

In his words, in his voice, in his eyes, she saw reflected the love between his parents and him.

"So your father goes to court like Perry Mason?"

"Doubt it's like Perry Mason. But he's had some big cases, at least for Wyoming."

"Do you go see him in court?"

"Mom took us once as kids, but we got kicked out."

She raised her head. "*Both* of you?"

He grinned. "Both, yes, but not my sister and me—Mom and me. Actually, Dad asked for a brief recess, then came back to where we were sitting in our best clothes, and said Amy could stay if she wanted, but he couldn't stand the silent screams of boredom from Mom and me, so would we please go back to the ranch, get on a horse, and ride out our fidgets."

She laughed. "He sounds like a wonderful man."

"I suppose he is. He's a lot quieter than Mom. She told me once that she couldn't be who she is if he weren't who he is. I thought about that when you were telling me about your parents."

"That's lovely. And I think my parents would say that, too. You know, now that you've proven you can sit still and watch a musical, I bet you can sit and watch your dad in court. You should do that."

"I suppose I should." He sounded thoughtful.

Satisfied, she put her head down, and said, "Tell me about a typical day at the Slash-C."

"Not much typical about any day. Changes season to season, and day to day. So it depends on which day."

"January sixteenth," she said.

"Okay, let's see. Mid-January…"

She could have listened to him talk about anything, but to see his ranch in his words, to hear his love for the land in his voice was something she knew she would carry inside always.

She picked dates at random, and heard about fence repairs, calving, branding, moving the herd, haying. There was so much, with contingencies for sick animals or mechanical failures or neighbors needing help or flood, blizzard, drought, grassfires—and those were only the ones she remembered—that she wasn't sure he was done until he'd been quiet for a while.

Then, she said, "And you say I work hard."

He chuckled, the rumble absorbed through her cheek, and into her soul. "I had a girlfriend in college—"

"A serious girlfriend?"

He considered that, as he so often did when answering her, being sure he told her the truth. "Serious enough. Hey, don't get that perfect little nose of yours out of joint—"

"I don't have my nose out of joint," she disputed, while also relishing his calling her extremely ordinary nose *perfect*.

"You wrinkled it hard enough to knock it out of joint."

"You're trying to wriggle out of telling me some deep dark secret about this girlfriend."

"Nothing deep or dark or secret. She just didn't understand about the Slash-C. She said she did, but she didn't. I knew that when she started saying how fun it would be to take off for *impromptu* vacations several times a year. Like we could just up and leave the animals to care for themselves, the work to do itself. You've got to plan ahead, get somebody in, ask some favors."

"But—" She bit it off.

He stroked her hair. "Yeah, you're right. But that's what I did for these extra days. I know."

His voice deepened and roughened on the last two words, a tone that opened a door to a new dimension between them.

She backed away. "Maybe she wanted to be sure you rested enough, this wonderful girlfriend of yours."

After a pause, he picked up the same tone. "Nah. She thought she'd catch herself a rich ranch owner at the University of Wyoming, and all she got was me. For a while."

"She *was* right that you should get away sometimes, everyone needs that. And when you do, you should make the most of it."

He nuzzled her neck, and rumbled. "I thought we were."

She felt a blush rising.

As if his lips sensed the heat, he looked up. His smile, satisfied and promising, sparked a new pulsing, deep in her belly.

"We have to take a break some time," she said. To him? Or to remind herself? "If we get dressed now, we can walk to the theater, then after the matinee—"

"Sorry, I'm not coming to the matinee."

She paused in the process of getting out of bed, looking over her shoulder at him. He'd been at so many performances, and with the stock show closed … But she shouldn't have assumed. "Oh."

"I've, uh, I've got a sort of appointment."

"Okay. But I need to get going. I'll take a quick shower. Alone," she added as he moved as if to get up. "It'll be faster."

Done with her shower, standing in front of the sink, a towel wrapped around her as she cleansed her face, she let her thoughts surface enough to recognize them.

Whatever he was hiding from her, it wouldn't hurt her. Except that it did push against that fragile bubble surrounding them.

She was rinsing her face when she felt him come up behind her. As she straightened, he kissed her shoulder.

"I'm sorry I won't be there this afternoon." He met her gaze in the mirror. "Don't look like that, Donna. I'll be there tonight for sure."

That wasn't the cause of her frown. The frown was for her thoughts.

Whatever he was hiding from her, it wouldn't hurt her.

She knew he wouldn't hurt her, like she knew the rain came from the sky and plants grew toward the sun. She trusted him. Completely. After so few days. And with even fewer days until they parted.

Leaning forward to turn off the faucet, she caught his expression in the mirror, and stilled.

Slowly, she straightened. She reached back with one hand and cupped his face, while her other hand loosed the towel and let it drop.

Under her fingertips, the pulse in his neck jumped.

Watching her, his hands came up and cupped her breasts. So absolutely right...

She arched, pressing herself into the perfect hold of his palms. He buried his mouth into the curve of her shoulder and throat, sucking lightly, as his fingers and thumbs stroked and teased her nipples.

She rested back against him, feeling his erection, watching the flush of desire rise up her body, seeing her nipples darken and peak as he must have seen them. Wanting him. Needing—

She turned. Rupturing one connection, but intending to gain so much.

With her hands on his chest, she nudged him backward, as she kissed him with a passion fueled by exultation and, despite herself, sorrow.

Back, step by step, across the bathroom threshold, to the bed.

He dropped to the mattress, wrapping her securely in his arms to take her with. When he would have turned them she resisted.

She straddled his hips. His hands came back to her breasts. But when she took him in her hands, he said, "Donna?" And gripped her waist.

She dropped and he was inside her—

His hips came up off the bed in response.

—completely.

"Donna," Lydia stopped her in the backstage corridor with a hand to her arm.

"Sorry, I don't have time—"

"I'm worried about—"

"No need to worry, I'll pay my share of the room."

"That's *not* what I'm worried about. You're going to be hurt. You've spent every minute—"

"I've gotta go." She couldn't bear to hear about ships passing in the night, about not getting entangled. Not now.

What had gotten into her? She knew the risks. She *knew*. She was always cautious. Always. A pregnancy and her career could be—would be—over. So, why could she not regret that moment?

"Donna..." Lydia's voice and concern trailed after her.

She turned the corner to the stubby corridor that held Maudie's room, but saw Grover slipping in the door, and halted.

She didn't want to talk with the stage door keeper any more than she'd wanted to talk to Lydia.

As she pivoted away, Henri snagged her arm. "C'mon, let's get out of here," he said with a hint of twang instead of his usual accent.

"Henri, I don't want to—"

"Me, either. We'll go find a burger joint, eat all the stuff we shouldn't and not say a thing."

Henri kept his word. Yet she felt the strain on the bubble—his unhappiness pushing against it from the outside, her dread scratching at it from the inside.

She just wanted these last days with Ed in peace. Every hour. Every minute.

He was there for the evening performance. She knew as soon as she came on stage.

Now he stood at the stage door, waiting for her.

She would slip back into the bubble. Ed would keep it whole and safe. She could rely on him for that.

For now.

CHAPTER SIXTEEN

Friday

Donna dropped her brush on the scarred makeup table.

"You used my brush again, didn't you, Lydia," she demanded.

"When would I have a chance to use it? You carry it back and forth in your bag, and you're never in our room because you're always off with your cowboy."

"Rancher," she snapped.

"He wears the hat, he's a cowboy. Not that I'm complaining, since I'm getting a single room at half the price."

Donna ignored all that, refusing to think about Ed's room, Ed's bed. "You must have used it in here then, because it's clogged with long blonde hairs with dark roots."

Nora barked out a laugh. "Listen to yourself, Columbo. You'd have to arrest the entire cast. You're just in a funk because you broke the simplest rule—you let yourself fall for a local."

"Nora—" warned Lydia. She had a roommate's prerogative to chastise. Nora didn't.

"And I don't care if he is good-looking or the best—"

"Shut up," added MaryBeth.

"—you've had. You're an idiot. You could have just had good sex, but you try to make it something more. You had to—"

Donna raised the brush.

"—go and fall in—"

Henri came from nowhere, wrapped his arms around Nora, and yanked her out of the room like a hawk with a mouse before Donna fully assimilated that he was there.

Into the frozen silence Maudie calmly arrived, taking Nora's now empty seat.

Donna turned her back on the room, facing the mirror, seeing nothing, yet aware of looks zinging around the room behind her.

"Boy, did you see the snow today?" said a voice Donna didn't bother to identify.

Eager affirmative murmurs followed.

"—hardly see my hand in front of my face—"

"—Nearly froze—"

"—slipped into a puddle—"

"—looks like Christmas."

The last comment drew a new flurry of comments.

"—decorations—"

"—found a present—"

"—haven't started shopping—"

"—getting in the Christmas mood."

"Me, too. Christmas in San Francisco, that'll be fun. I can hardly wait," Raeanne said.

Donna focused on her makeup.

"Don't you think, Donna? The cable cars and—"

"We'll be onstage. Doesn't matter where we are."

Donna knew she'd snapped. Knew that everyone in the dressing room looked at her again. Then at each other. She wiped off eyeliner and started again.

"Yes, well, in the meantime," Maudie said. "We're here in Denver, and it's being very good to us. Another full house tonight."

The chatter resumed, no longer about the schedule.

Doesn't matter where we are.

That was the issue, wasn't it?

Because wherever they were, Ed Currick wouldn't be there.

"Tell me about snowberries, Ed."

"You want to talk about vegetation?" Implicit was the added question: *Now?*

"Yes," she said firmly.

They'd made love twice since returning to the hotel.

If she were ever asked the highlight of Denver, Colorado, she could never top this room in the Rockton Hotel.

"All right. Snowberry's a bush. Not real big. Like I told you, it reminds me of you."

"Hey," she protested, yet loving his chuckle.

"I'm just telling you, like you asked. As I was saying before you interrupted, it's—"

"Short. I got it, Ed. I've already heard all the lines—stumpy legs, sawed off, when are you going to stand up?"

"I wouldn't say short," he said judiciously. "More like it mixes in well with other bushes, doesn't tower over them, keeps their spirits up."

She grinned at that.

"It's happiest a little higher up, right along where timber starts. Maybe if a stringer of pines grows down a ridge, it comes along. Only on northern slopes. Sometimes down in a gully, especially if it's fed by a stream. They don't like getting dried out, and that's what would happen on a south-facing slope. Southern slope would make no sense at all."

"Okay, never on a southern slope," she said slowly. Where was this vehemence coming from? As if he were arguing the point. "Does it bloom?"

"Yeah. In the spring."

He sounded grim, which made even less sense than his vehemence.

"Are the blooms pretty?" she ventured.

"Sure. They hang down in a clump. Look sort of like narrow bells, like in Christmas decorations. Only, instead of red and green and gold, snowberry's bells are white and pink and ... in between."

His gaze had dropped to where she held the sheet over her breasts.

"And then the blossoms turn into those smooth, white berries."

His wonderful voice lingered over the final words, while his gaze never shifted. She felt her nipples pushing at the sheet. She sucked in a breath.

He kept talking in that low, almost hypnotic way.

"The clusters of flowers become clusters of berries that stick around well into winter—must be where they got their name. Because the berries are white and they're still around in the snow. Not the best forage for cattle, but lots of small wildlife and birds wouldn't make it through winter without snowberry. Snowberry feeds them and snowberry shelters them. Takes them in with open arms and makes them feel like they've never felt."

He slowly raised his head, bringing his gaze to hers. The air in her lungs heated, caught fire.

"Makes them feel like they've never felt before," he repeated.

She knew what he was saying. She knew what he felt. She felt it, too.

But if they went too far down that road…

She tried a smile. "And then the, uh, the birds and the wildlife move on. Happy to have had that time. That—" She cleared her throat. "—magical time. Grateful. But knowing they were moving on, while the snowberry … wasn't." He'd said snowberry reminded him of her, but *she* was the wildlife, *he* was the snowberry. "Because it grew in that spot, drawing strength from the land through deep, deep roots."

Tears glazed her eyes, but she didn't let them fall. She looked at him, letting him see into her, looking into him. It was all there in that look.

All that they couldn't have.

"Christmas music," he said abruptly.

Even as she blinked at the harshness in his voice, she recognized what he was doing.

She should be glad. But she didn't want to play their game. She wanted—No. She couldn't. It wasn't his fault. It wasn't her fault. It just was.

"Perry Como," she said after a long moment.

"Bing Crosby."

"Nat King Cole."

"The Chipmunks."

That snapped her out of robot mode. "Really? The Chipmunks"

"Sure. 'Christmas Don't Be Late.' I sing it to the cattle."

"Surprised you haven't started stampedes."

"Who says I haven't?"

She grinned. Creaky, but a real grin. She suspected Ed Currick could make her grin under any circumstances if he set his mind to it. " 'Oh, Holy Night.' "

" 'All I Want For Christmas Are My Two Front Teeth.' "

He settled against the headboard, circled her with one arm and drew her in, so her head rested on his shoulder.

" 'What Child Is This,' " she said.

"The weather outside is frightful."

"That's called 'Winter Wonderland.' "

"I like the part about Parson Brown, marrying them when they're in town."

She tried to look at him without moving her head, but all she saw was his chin. She swallowed. "Which carols don't you like?"

" 'Blue Christmas.' You?"

" 'I Saw Mommy Kissing Santa Claus'—I foresee therapy in that child's future."

"Good point. My favorite was 'I'll Be Home for Christmas' until I found out what it's about—a World War II soldier who can't be home for Christmas and dreams about it."

She sat up. "It is?"

"Yup. Your guy Bing made it during World War II."

"But the dreaming helps him. Or…" She thought of the undercurrent of melancholy in the words. "Or maybe it's better not to dream."

CHAPTER SEVENTEEN

Saturday

They'd lost track of time while figuring out a new way to make love in the shower without flooding the bathroom.

A cab got them to the theater just in time for her to make call for the matinee.

With time to kill before he joined the audience, he went to a drugstore and found a phone booth.

"Slash-C," his father's voice came.

"Dad."

"Ed? Are you o—Is everything okay? You sound, uh, tired."

"Everything's okay. Just wanted…" What did he want that anyone could give him? He wanted Donna. He wanted Donna to be happy. He didn't want to imagine walking in a world where Donna wasn't happy.

Since that college girlfriend, he'd been sure he'd marry a ranch girl. Someone who knew his way of life. Knew the land, the animals.

Donna didn't know any of that.

He closed his eyes and saw the Slash-C, and she was there.

On a horse, laughing down at him. Sitting beside him on one of his favorite rocks, looking out across the land. Standing on the home ranch's back porch, waving to him as he rode out for the day. Standing on the porch, welcoming him home at night.

No matter what he did now, he couldn't see it without her.

He'd never marry a ranch girl.

"Ed?" his father said.

"I'll be home Monday night, like I told you. Just wanted to let you know."

Between performances, they ate at the little Mexican restaurant again.

Not the best choice before a performance, but it didn't matter because she ate very little. They talked even less.

She tried a few times.

Bright, Ado Annie comments about the food, the season, the weather. The weather for heaven's sake. What did she care? Unless a blizzard or monsoon or hurricane roared in and kept the company and Ed marooned here. Days, weeks, years, like Robinson Crusoe, except they'd be together.

Everyone was checking their makeup for the last time, taking that final breath before "places" for the evening performance when Angela appeared at the doorway in full Charity regalia.

That was the first surprise, since she usually ran right up to, sometimes past, the time she needed to be on stage.

"This afternoon's show was not up to standard," she announced.

That silenced the surprised murmurs at her arrival. She was wrong, for one thing. Plus, she never commented on performances. As far as anyone could tell, she wasn't aware of what anyone else did on stage. Henri said she acted from inside a glass booth.

Angela's gaze raked down the row of those at the communal makeup table, flicked to Nora, then to Donna. It stayed there as she moved to behind Donna, leaning over, as if needing the mirror to adjust an eyebrow hair with a fingernail.

"Donna, if you hope to push out Nora and grab that Helene role, you need to hit your cues. Very sloppy. You've let yourself be distracted by that country bumpkin cowboy. Screw whoever you want, but don't let it show on stage."

She met Donna's gaze in the mirror for an instant, then picked up the brush.

Before Angela completed a first step toward the door, Donna stood, jostling her with a hip on the way up, and snatched back the brush.

"You're wrong, Angela. On every point. This afternoon's performance was one of the best by all members of this company except one. I hit my cues perfectly, as well as my marks. I am not taking the role of Helene—or as you called her today, *Ellen*—Lydia is. I am going to play Nikki. And Nora is leaving us for an excellent role in an upcoming movie."

Donna didn't even have a chance to utter a prayer that the backstage gossip about Nora's future was right before the "places!" call echoed through the open doorway.

She pivoted away from open-mouthed Angela, walked to the door, where Maudie waited—as always, on hand during a crisis—and handed her the brush with a low, "Guard this with your life."

With the best timing she'd ever shown, Nora rose, said, "Donna's got that right," and fell in line behind her. Then Lydia, MaryBeth, and Raeanne.

But Donna hadn't left the doorway yet. "And, finally, Ed Currick of the Slash-C Ranch in Knighton, Wyoming, is not a country bumpkin. He is a rancher. He is *my* rancher. And the *lovemaking* is better than you could ever imagine."

Then she marched out. Followed by the others.

Their shared air of triumph was slightly diminished when Brad hissed that they were supposed to be world-weary taxi dancers, not ready to take on the Russian army, and they all had to concentrate on finding their Fandango Ballroom slouch before the curtain rose.

Whispered "Atta girls" came at Donna in under-their-breath snatches throughout the performance, drifted from dark shadows where crew members toiled, and even rose up from the orchestra.

Maudie stopped her after the last curtain call, drawing her into her room, though neither of them sat.

"Don't tell me I shouldn't have said any of that to her," Donna said.

"I won't. But you will need to be careful now. On stage and back-stage. If you want to succeed."

"I don't ca-." She caught a gleam in Maudie's eyes and bit it off.

The older woman didn't challenge her, instead saying, "A milque-toast does not succeed in this business. Standing up for yourself is good if you want to go to the top. But you are now targeted as a potential threat to her ambitions, since yours are the same."

That last phrase might have held a question, but Donna felt no obligation to answer.

Only Nora remained in the dressing room when Donna began the high-speed makeup removal routine she'd perfected since arriving in Denver.

She had her coat half on as she passed Nora's table, but the other woman's hand on her arm stopped her.

"Thank you. I know—Well. But you reminded me tonight that I used to be you. Nice."

Donna swallowed. Nora had been catty and waspish and some-times downright unpleasant, and she wasn't exactly apologizing. Still ... "I wish you well, Nora."

The usual mocking smile returned. "I do, too—wish me well."

Donna nodded, accepting the thank you ... and the other woman's limitations.

Grover was nowhere to be seen, but as soon as Donna opened the exterior door, she spotted Lydia talking fast to Ed, whose gaze had already zeroed in on her.

Lydia turned, following the direction of Ed's look, said one last thing, then waved at Donna and hurried down the alleyway to catch up with the others.

Ed brought Donna to him with one arm, lowered his head and kissed her thoroughly.

When they both had to breathe, he said, "I hear you defended my honor. Thank you."

She sighed. "Lydia."

"Oh, no, she was the latecomer to the party. I'd heard about it from the minute I showed up back here. Grover, stagehands, a woman from the orchestra I don't know, and Henri came out still in full makeup to fill me in on *Killer Donna.* According to him, you called me a stud and—"

"I did *not*—"

"—said Angela should be so lucky."

"Well, I did sort of imply that."

He laughed, tightened his hold, and kissed her even more thoroughly.

This time when the paltry need for oxygen forced their mouths apart, he said, "I have something for you."

She looked quickly to his face, saw the pleasure there. Then down, and saw a small box in his hands.

She sucked in a breath.

A jewelry box. A jewelry—*oh my God*...

No—not a jewelry box. At least not *that* kind of jewelry. Wrong shape. More like a box for a necklace. Wrapped in blue paper with an inexpertly manipulated gold ribbon and bow.

A somewhat chunky necklace, come to think of it.

The box tipped in Ed's hands, and whatever was inside slid to one end with a sound that didn't seem quite right for a necklace.

She looked into eyes that had lost their smile, replaced by uncertainty.

"Donna—?"

"For me?" she asked. She couldn't let him ask about her reaction. She couldn't even think about it herself. "What is it?"

The box leveled off, and his smile edged back. "That's what unwrapping's for."

He extended it, and she took it, smiling at his pleasure, shutting away any other reaction.

One tug and the ribbon untied. Then she tore at the paper.

"Ah, you're one of those unwrappers, huh?" he teased.

"You expected me to delicately peel away one corner at a time?"

"Not for a second."

She ignored his chuckle, tossing the paper, and taking the top off the box.

It took an extra beat, blinking down at what she held.

"Buttons?" She said the word more to confirm her recognition of the flat, round objects than to draw an answer. "Oh ... Oh! *My* buttons. The buttons for my coat. Are these—? They *are*. The original designer buttons. How on earth did you—where did you—?"

"It took some doing," he admitted. "It was mostly Maudie. She gave me a list of places to look Thursday afternoon, and wherever I went and mentioned her name they'd dug into every last corner, trying to find what I was after. It was a longshot, but we hit it."

"Maudie. Ah, so *that's* what you two were conspiring about the other night."

"Yup. Was afraid you'd worm it out of me right then. And I was afraid you'd notice we took a button from your sleeve."

"My sleeve?" Her fingers went to the cuff.

He grinned. "Other one. You touch this one a lot, and I figured you'd notice. So I asked Maudie to take it from the other one."

"Oh!" She switched to the other sleeve and her fingers immediately discovered two buttons instead of three. "Maudie cut it off? You two *were* conspiring."

"Only so you can sew on those buttons and—"

"And have a perfect coat. Thank you, Ed. Thank you so much." She sighed with huge satisfaction. "My coat will be absolutely perfect."

"I was going to say you can sew on those buttons and stay warm."

She laughed. "I will, I will. But for now ... Would you rather I sew on buttons? Or shall we find another way to stay warm?"

CHAPTER EIGHTEEN

Sunday

No sewing was accomplished Saturday night.

After making love, they fell asleep. But when he woke in the early morning he seemed to know she was awake, too.

He kissed her hair, and said, "Egg nog."

"Hot coffee with cinnamon, and whipped cream."

"Mulled cider."

"Hot-buttered—" Her voice broke. "Hold me, Ed. Please, just hold me."

He held her. As night lifted and the December daylight found them.

There was no mention of what the passing time was leading to. Even as they packed, quickly, badly, in the short time left before she needed to leave for the finale's special five o'clock curtain.

Only when she was four feet from the stage door did she stop and turn to him. "Will you—?"

"I'll be here after the show," he said. It sounded grim. "I'll be here."

She nodded. Their bubble was stretched to its limits.

She went up on tiptoe and he came down to her for a kiss. His tongue claimed hers with a rhythm and heat that was theirs. She clung to him. Wanting to sob, but unwilling to waste seconds of this kiss on something so useless.

"It's final call, Donna!" Grover's shout came as if from far away. "Get in here, girl!"

She spun away, not letting herself look back, moving automatically into the routines of a last show.

She sensed Ed in the audience, as always. But it didn't buoy her this time.

Something else got her through that performance. Professionalism, or the audience's enthusiasm, or self-protective numbness. She floated through it without once connecting with the reality of the moment. Even when the curtain came down for the last time after enthusiastic curtain calls from the Denver theater-goers applauding their thanks and farewells.

Farewells...

Yes, that is what she would wish Ed. That he fare well always. Always.

"C'mon, Donna! Lots to do. Let's go, let's go, let's go," barked Brad. And she realized she was standing alone, the rest of the company streaming toward the dressing rooms to get out of costumes and makeup and into their departure day routines to head—

She didn't know where. She didn't care.

The bus was in the alley behind the theater. If he looked down this side-alley toward the back, he could see workers moving around, packing up.

Ed didn't look that way. He kept his eyes on the stage door, and his mind blank.

The door opened. Grover gave him a quick salute, then looked back into the building.

The doorkeeper barely had time to move aside before Donna came flying out. Ed met her, engulfed her in his arms, even as he turned her away from the interested gazes of those waiting for mundane autographs.

"Ed—"

He stopped her words with a kiss, now that he had her in a shadowed spot beyond the stage door.

He tasted the sorrow on her lips. He was beyond caring what she might taste on his.

They kissed, and kissed. Their bodies aligning themselves for what they most wanted to do this very instant. Her buttonless coat swung open, eliminating one obtrusive layer of clothing.

She unbuttoned his jacket, burrowing inside it, so they pressed that much closer together.

Then her hands pulled at his shirt at the back of his waist, finding his skin, and he did the same at her waist. So there, just there and where their mouths met, they were skin to skin, as they longed to be everywhere.

The bus horn blasted twice this time. She'd ignored the first, single warning. This one she couldn't.

Donna broke from him.

"I have to—" She clamped her mouth closed, afraid her next sound would be a wail.

He spun around, grabbed her hand and headed toward the bus, with her in tow. Moving so fast that she half stumbled, trying to keep up.

His hold kept her from falling, but he didn't slow.

And then they were there. Just beyond a shifting clump of humanity beginning to send individuals up the bus steps, one by one.

"Everybody on the bus, let's go, let's go, let's go." Even Brad's bark was muted in the nighttime chill.

Ed put an arm around her, carrying her bag in his other hand. "I should have gotten the buttons sewed on for you. If that damned coat had buttons on it, you wouldn't be shivering."

Yes she would.

It was now. Right now.

The moment she'd known would come from the beginning.

She smiled brightly. "It's been wonderful, Ed. I'll never for—" She couldn't finish the word. "One of those ships passing in the night romances that you remember always, but—"

"That's not what this is and we both know it," he snapped.

She sucked in a breath and looked up. That was a mistake. She couldn't maintain the pretense when she looked at him.

"Is it?" he demanded.

She shook her head. The motion loosed a tear from her bottom lashes and let it slide down her cheek.

"Let's be honest about this. I can't do what I do or be who I am except at the Slash-C. And you can't do what you do or be who you are except on the stage, isn't that right?"

Miserable, she nodded, releasing more tears. Even as a voice inside her cried, *I don't know.*

"So, I'm going to kiss you one more time, and then I'm going. But we both know what this is. And we both know what's ending now."

He didn't ask a question. She prevented that voice inside her from forming any answer.

She stretched to meet his kiss, arms wrapped around his strong neck. All that mattered was absorbing the feel of him, the taste of him into every pore, so she would always have this with her. Always.

The kiss ended, both of them breathing hard, hers with ragged edges that sank toward sobs.

" 'They Can't Take That Away From Me'—from us—isn't that what that song says?" he said, no longer harsh.

Amid the welter of emotions inside her, she heard the melody of that sweet, sad song, heard the lyrics of a lover's memories that would be held forever.

"You have changed my life," he said. "I love you, Donna."

Then he turned and strode away.

And she let him go, their bubble burst.

CHAPTER NINETEEN

December 22

"—are you listening to me, Ed?"

He looked up from the breakfast table to where his mother stood at the door, gloves in hand, otherwise dressed to step outside.

"Fence. Battery Creek today. Back Ridge tomorrow," he said.

She huffed. "Well, don't be all day about it."

"I won't."

She propped her hands on her hips. Her glare made no dent.

"I don't know what's gotten into you since Denver. Staying on like you'd never come back, then driving all night as if you couldn't get away fast enough. Foolish. It's not like you. Are you sick?"

"No."

She huffed again. She swung around, eager to get on with problems she could solve, then called over her shoulder, "Have a good day in court, Walt," and was out the door.

Ed's unfocused gaze returned to the table surface.

"Don't be fooled by looks." His father's words were unexpected enough to make him look up again.

Anger shot through him. No one was going to dismiss Donna Roberts that way, like all he'd fallen for were her looks. He wouldn't listen to that, not even from—

Reason caught up.

His father knew nothing about Donna, much less having an opinion about her.

"Lots of people are fooled by how much you look like your mother, don't you be, too," his father said.

Now he was really confused. "What?"

Walter Edward Currick shook out his newspaper and folded it along its creases. Only when they were perfect did he continue. "Your looks, and your love for the Slash-C, that's what folks see. But you know why you get along so well with your mother? Not because you're exactly alike, but because you aren't. You're my son, too."

He looked into his father's eyes. Seeing love there and understanding, but no inclination to relent.

"She's worried about you," his father said. "How you've been since you came back. She doesn't understand."

And you think you do? The challenge shot through his mind, followed immediately by repentance. How could his father or anyone understand when Ed didn't.

He kept silent. Usually his father took the hint.

Not this time. "You know the story of how your mother and I met, you know how your grandmother and grandfather met. First sight at a party, and that was it, first for your grandfather, then for me. And you're a Currick, through and through."

They looked across the table at each other.

Ed recognized his father's strength in a courtroom. Not as a distant, theoretical matter, but something real. The draw to answer the unspoken question was so strong…

Ed pounded the side of his fist on the table, making the dishes, salt shaker, and newspaper—but not his father—jump.

"Not this time, damn it. No happy ending for this Currick after love at first sight."

The *damn it* hadn't released any of his frustration. He added a stream of curses.

They didn't help, either. He wound down to silence, his father still looking at him.

He jerked out of his chair, strode to the door, and flung it open with a force that set the hinges screeching. But before it slammed closed with him on the other side, he stepped back in and caught the door.

"Why do you stay if you hate it?"

His father's eyebrows rose. "Hate what?"

"Here. The ranch. The life."

Only when the echo of those harsh words died did his father speak. "The *life*—ranching—isn't for me. It's not the challenge that sets my blood to pumping the way it does for you and your mother. The *ranch*, I have a great deal of fondness for and I value the continuity and connection." His voice turned wry. "I do, however, recognize there are places of interest beyond the Slash-C. Unlike your mother and you. At least…?"

His expression made it more a question than his voice. This time Ed withstood the draw to respond.

His father picked up smoothly, "*Here?* Ah, *here* is what really matters. *Here* is where the people I love live the lives they love, so *here* is where I belong, all other factors aside."

He would never have that. Weight pressed harder against Ed's chest. This time, not only had he been thrown, but the horse, the bull, the tractor had landed on top of him. Best he could hope was to crawl out from under someday.

He pivoted in the doorway.

"Ed."

Reluctantly, he faced his father.

"To have a happy ending, first you need a happy start and—"

"Impossible." He didn't think he had any more words, but that one shot out.

"—not even that comes right all the time. Sometimes you have to work to reach the happy start. Your mother and I did. When I was your age, I wanted nothing more than to see the last of the Slash-C. Was going to be a city dweller come hell or high water. Had to adjust my thinking. About my life, about her life. More than that, I had to realize it wasn't that I wanted to live in a city and not be on the ranch, it was that I wanted the law, rather than ranching. Hasn't worked out too bad, all in all."

The understatement of a man supremely happy with his life and his wife.

"It's not part of the story that gets told, but it took nearly two years for your mother and me to really come together, Ed. Two years of talking and arguing and testing our feelings."

Ed stared at the floor.

No, his stare wasn't at the floor. It was at his father's boots.

Nice boots. Good enough for court, as his mother's comment had indicated Walt Currick had today. Yet not so fancy they forgot the ranch. A man who'd found a way to straddle two worlds.

"Not possible," Ed said after some time. "Not possible."

"Because of who the girl is—?"

"*No!*"

His father went on without a pause, "I take it she returns your feelings. Yes, I see." Though what he saw Ed couldn't imagine. His father steepled his fingers in a familiar gesture. "You won't leave the Slash-C, so I can only imagine she won't or can't come here. Ah, yes … Well, then, Ed, what you need to do is to turn that good mind of yours to this problem. Since *who* and *what* and *why* are the givens, and *where* is the hurdle, what's left are *how* and *when.*"

"Everyone has gone," Maudie said from the doorway. It was an accusation.

Tonight's party to celebrate the opening of an extended run in San Francisco was at a nearby restaurant. Very posh, everyone had said as they bustled out.

"I wasn't in the mood."

"Again."

"Yes."

Maudie came and stood behind her. It seemed the other woman's will forced Donna to lift her head, to lock gazes in the mirror.

"You, who are so happy, were miserable at Thanksgiving, but that was a day, two. This has been too long. You must talk—"

"I don't want to talk—to you or Lydia or anyone."

"Ah, so Lydia is worried, as well. She has a good heart, though not the best of heads. What you should think about—"

"I don't want to think. I want to do my job and be left alone."

Maudie ignored her. "Your *job*. Yes. Not *life* for you."

"You're saying because I miss my family at Thanksgiving and Christmas that I'm not cut out for theater? Is that what you're—?"

The older woman's *Tch* silenced her. "You cannot listen to reason when you're talking such nonsense."

Maudie left, and Donna returned to absently cleaning her makeup brushes. A far more productive use of time than a party.

Eventually she'd have to attend opening night parties again. Not yet.

The only true pang she felt was about Henri. Brad had broken up with him two days ago upon their arrival in San Francisco, reportedly reconnecting with a previous lover. She hadn't been much of a friend to Henri these past days.

She hadn't been much of anything.

The new role had required learning lyrics, blocking, lines. She'd welcomed that work. Relied on it. Threw herself into it with the hope each day that she would be too tired by night to do anything but sleep. She was never tired enough.

Everyone seemed pleased with her performances.

But she knew that if Stan Henson came back and saw her, the director would not talk about glow and joy.

She had left those in Denver.

No, they had gone to somewhere she'd never been—Knighton, Wyoming.

CHAPTER TWENTY

December 23

Ed straightened. The fence repair would hold until they dug new post holes come spring. The sweat of exertion cooled under his layers of clothes, his muscles relaxing.

He looked out at the land he knew so well. It was in his blood—his mouth twisted—and his blood was in it, including some drops today from a barb that had slipped through his work gloves.

Blood, sweat and tears put into this land. And it gave back.

It was as much a part of his family as his parents, his sister, his grandparents.

You know the story … First sight at a party, and that was it, first for your grandfather, then for me.

He'd heard those stories all his life. Yesterday was the first time he'd heard about the two years that had followed first sight.

He wished he'd been hearing *that* all his life. One thing for sure, if he ever did get married and have a kid, he wouldn't tell them some family legend of falling in love at first sight.

Not now that he knew what could happen after that first sight.

Since who *and* what *and* why *are the givens, and* where *is the hurdle, what's left are* how *and* when.

If he had any idea what his father had meant he'd be thinking like hell about it. *How* and *when.* What would that get him—get them, him and Donna.

Donna. His heart clutched like a muscle strained past endurance.

What was she doing right now? Tomorrow was Christmas Eve,

would she be doing any of the things they'd talked about in Denver? Was she happy this Christmas?

He looked out again. At the land he loved so deeply.

He'd never before viewed it as empty. Or as lonely.

CHAPTER TWENTY-ONE

December 25

The urgent need to sew the buttons onto her coat provided Donna an excuse to decline an invitation to join the rest of the company for a Christmas night celebration.

It wasn't a great excuse.

Especially since they'd also wanted to celebrate her first performance as Charity.

Angela had called in "sick." Rumor was she'd left San Francisco and had flown to Los Angeles for either a rendezvous with a lover or to try to get a role in an upcoming movie. Or both.

As a result, Donna had played the lead role in the national touring company of "Sweet Charity," in one of the biggest theaters on their tour. The spotlight she'd dreamed of had been trained on her. She'd been great.

Everybody said so. Everybody exulted at it. Even she knew she'd done an exceptional job. Hardly any nerves at all.

So, yes, her excuse had drawn a few rolled eyes. But she'd stuck to it.

After all, she needed to get these buttons on. She needed the warmth against San Francisco's raw, foggy chill, since she didn't have anyone walking beside her buffering her from it.

Maudie had supplied her with needle, thread and scissors. The mindless task suited Donna. Mindless meant no mind, and no mind meant no thinking. That was good. All good.

A knock sounded on the frame to the open dressing room door.

"Come in," she said, though Barker, the doorman, had already shambled across the threshold. Another city, another theater, another doorman. This one actually opened the door sometimes.

She preferred Grover.

She put the needle through the fabric and pulled the thread steadily.

"You got one," Barker said.

Donna's head snapped up. "*What?*"

She spun around to Maudie, pinning a note about repairs to a costume at the back of the communal dressing room.

Maudie shook her head, and raised her hands, denying any knowledge.

"Not one of those hippies, neither. He asked me to ask you—"

"No. Send him away. I won't see him. I won't see anyone."

Barker looked past her to Maudie. From the corner of her eye, Donna caught Maudie's shrug.

Barker turned and left.

Not another word was said until Donna clipped the last thread on the last button, and shook out her coat.

Maudie came and tucked the sewing things into a bag hooked to her belt, then sat on the chair facing Donna. "Have you called him?"

"No."

"Has he called you?"

"No. We said everything already. He told me he loves his ranch. I told him my dream is to star on Broadway."

Maudie nodded. "That is the dream—the only dream—for some. Me, I just wanted a home and family." Her voice turned dreamy. "A little girl. Would've named her Lisa. Always liked that name. Lisa…"

"Then why—?"

"Why am I rattling around theaters as an old lady? I fell in love with Manny." She sighed. "Lord, he was beautiful. A principal dancer."

Donna felt a stab of envy, quick and sharp. Maudie's love had been of the theater, too. They'd had the chance to pursue their dreams together—She pushed that envy away. It was not only sharp, but poisonous.

"We were best of friends. Laughed, my how we laughed. Told each other everything." Maudie looked up, a sheen across faded brown eyes. "He was gay—queer they called it then. He never hid it from me, and when I told him I loved him anyway, he was the one held me while I cried my heart out."

Donna remembered Maudie's words that first night Ed had waited for her.

What would you be wanting with one who didn't want that eventually? A lot of good he'd do you.

Poor Maudie, to spend her life loving a man who could not love her back.

Ed loved her back. They just couldn't be together. Was that any better?

I can't do what I do or be who I am except at the Slash-C. And you can't do what you do or be who you are except on the stage.

"We stayed best friends right to the end. Lost my Manny eight years ago. But I lost my chance at a little girl named Lisa a long, long time before that."

"I'm so sorry, Maudie."

Maudie patted her hand. "I know. I just don't want you to be sorry when you're my age. For a few, performing's what they need to keep the blood pumping. Broadway or Timbuktu, doesn't matter, as long as there's an audience. For some, only being a star will do. Many become bitter in the trying, *or* in the succeeding. For others, this life is a wonder, but it's not all they are. Then there are those where the stage is mostly an accident. Performing isn't their love, *doing* is. Singing, Dancing. An empty room's as good as Broadway. Only you can know which of those is you, Donna. Only you."

She'd been so sure. Always so sure. Yet tonight, when the spotlight had focused on her, there had been nothing like what she'd felt with Ed's look. Could the stage spotlight be an imitation?

"One more thing you should think of," Maudie continued. "What we are willing to fight for tells the most about what is important deep inside. You snapped about me questioning your devotion to your *job*. But think of this, Donna. Day after day you accept how Angela mistreats you onstage. Not once do you react, much less confront her. Even though it has been weeks now. What *do* you stand up to her about? The brush from your parents, and her words—mere words—about Ed."

Even if she could have spoken Donna didn't know what she would have said.

Maudie sighed. "So, you think about what you have found worth fighting for, and what you have not. But for now, you'd best get back to the hotel."

"I'll wait for—"

"No, no, I have a lot to do. I'm leaving the company next week."

"*What?*" Shock jerked her head up.

"December thirtieth. Starting a new life with the new year."

"But—But ... where are you going? Why? Are you—"

"Dying?" The woman chuckled. "No. I'm going back to Denver. Going to live in sin with Grover. At least for a while. If it works out, I might marry him."

"But why? You love the theater, the company—"

"Why should be obvious. That rascal Grover knows a thing or two about women. Always did fancy a younger man. And the man still can *move*."

She smiled, and Donna felt a blush rising, and felt the urge to whisper *Oh, my*, and fan herself, the way Henri had about Ed.... *Ed*.

"I'll still have the theater," Maudie was saying. "Going to work with the companies coming through, make settling in easier for them. As for loving the company, I realized that the ones I like the best are folks like you and Theresa, the ones who end up leaving. You have Barker call you a cab. I'll see you tomorrow."

With her mind, so long numb, trying to process Maudie's news, she let the older woman hurry her toward the door.

Absorbed in the strange, small luxury of buttoning her coat, letting her fingers linger on the buttons Ed had found for her, Donna opened the stage door to discover the day's drizzle had turned to deluge. In her umbrella-less state, she remembered Maudie's order to call a cab.

She turned to call to the doorman, but in the motion, she caught sight of a solitary figure standing in the rain.

Her heart lurched with knowledge. Her breath stopped with joy.

"Ed."

He said nothing, just looked up at her. Rain sluicing down off his cowboy hat, blown into his face. His eyes raw and dark.

Then he opened his arms, and she was down the steps, flying at him before reaching the bottom, wrapping herself around his tall, strong, wet frame.

"He said you wouldn't see me," he said between kisses. "He said you said to go away."

"I didn't know it was you. I didn't know."

"I couldn't go away. I drove straight through. Two days. I couldn't go away. I couldn't stay away. Not until—not until I tried—Donna, I love you."

"I love you, too. Oh, Ed, I do love you. I wanted to tell you that so much. But it didn't seem fair when I was saying—"

He tried to hold her away from him. She wouldn't let him, tightening her arms around his neck, her legs around his waist.

"I didn't say I love you before that last minute because I can't say it without wanting to ask—but I wouldn't let myself ask, because this is your dream. But I couldn't stay away, either."

"Oh, Ed." She hung on to him, feeling his realness all around her. And then she felt something else. She angled back to poke at a bulge in his coat where it covered his chest. Something crinkled. "What is this?"

"Damn. I forgot." He opened two buttons and pulled out a trio of wilting branches with clumps of white berries, tied with a red bow. "Snowberry. For you. Didn't want 'em to get wet, though that doesn't make sense now I think of it, since they stand out in all weather. It's just, they made me think of you and I wanted to protect..." He swallowed. "Well..."

"Oh, Ed." She took the branches from him and threw her arms

around his neck again. "You're my glow. You're my joy. You're what I'll fight for. What are we going to do?"

"Not sure I followed that, but from what Grover and Maudie said there aren't many doing these musicals real long, maybe till they're forty or so."

"Forty!"

"Yes," he said, firmly. "So I'll wait. Then we'll marry, have a family, be at the ranch. Until then, you dance, you sing. You go after that dream, and I'll wait. I'll come see you as much as I can."

"What if I can't have children when I'm forty?" That wasn't the objection she'd meant to make, but those were the words that came out.

"We'll adopt. Plenty of ways to have a family."

"Oh, Ed," she whispered, looking into his eyes from the bit of shelter his hat brim provided from the rain. She knew she kept saying it over and over, but his name made him real, not an illusion appearing after a long night of staring at a ceiling.

"And even then, it's not like once you're at the Slash-C you can't go anywhere ever again. I'd never keep you from trips—whenever you want. And we'll go places together after I retire."

"Retire!" She had a hard time imagining forty. Retirement was impossible.

"I know it's a long way off," he said fast, "but I will retire, Donna. I swear it. We'll save every week right from the start, so we can travel to all the places you want to see. With you, I'll want to see them, too. We'll have a son and we'll put the ranch in his hands, because it'll be going really good by then and—"

"What if we don't have a son?"

But even as she said it, she knew they would. A sturdy toddler with his father's smile, before he became a man any parents could be proud of.

Oh, my God, she knew because she'd *seen* him—their son. The toddler in that odd seeing-triple moment the very first night. And the older man? Was that her future Ed? Oh, how she hoped so.

"We might have a daughter," she added.

A Lisa. Yes, they would have a girl named Lisa.

He stopped. "A daughter," he said slowly. Then, even more slowly, that wonderful smile spread across his face. "Who looks like you. That would be—" He swallowed hard again.

She blinked against a sting in her eyes, but kept her voice firm. "And what if they—the son, the daughter—don't want to take over the ranch."

His smile faded. "Then we'd sell it. Should be worth enough by then so I can take you places you want to go."

She sucked in a breath. He would. He would sell his family ranch that meant so much to him. The last thing she ever wanted him to do, he would. For her.

"Ed, I need you to do something for me. Will you promise?"

He tried to look into her eyes, but she had dropped her chin so he couldn't.

"I promise to try my damnedest to do it for you, Donna."

She raised her face. "Ask me."

"What?"

"Ask me. What you drove two days to ask, ask me now."

"Donna—"

"You promised."

"But—"

"Ask me, Edward David Currick."

"I—"

"Ed—

"Okay, okay, I'm asking. Will you marry me, Donna? When you can—when you want to—will you be my wife?"

"Yes. And when I want to is forever. Starting right now."

"Now?"

"Now."

"But—"

"You've got to break this *but* habit, Ed. I'll marry you, and I'll be your wife at the Slash-C now, and I'll find ways to sing and dance, because I don't need a stage for that. And when you retire—and retire you will, I will not have you work yourself to death—we will go to many wonderful and exotic places together."

Maudie was right. She loved singing, she loved dancing. She didn't need an audience for that love to continue. But she needed Ed. And his love. This was what she would fight for. Always.

"Donna—"

"Now it's your turn to say yes."

He studied her, blinking through rain that slid past his hat brim, and perhaps tears, to look into her eyes.

"Yes," he said slowly. Then he smiled, and she knew she would never stop loving that smile. "Oh, hell, yes!"

He kissed her hard and deep, his arms around her no longer simply supporting her, but binding her to him. He tried to push her coat aside.

"What the hell?"

"I sewed on the buttons. Just now."

He grumbled a curse.

But eventually—hours after he had wrenched several off in his glorious hurry to get her out of her coat—he forgave those buttons. They were the only reason they made it back to her hotel room without giving an X-rated show that might have shocked even San Francisco.

EPILOGUE

Knighton, Wyoming—Present Day

"Donna, if you don't come now, we'll miss the flight."

"I know. As soon as I check the freezer—"

He caught her arm, preventing her returning to the house.

"Dave is too smart to starve. If he weren't, I'd be a damned idiot to leave him to run the ranch."

"Of course he's smart—he's brilliant," she said immediately, letting herself be led toward the pickup. Count on her to defend her kids from any whiff of criticism ... unless she was voicing it. "His law practice is going great and he'll keep the Slash-C running smoothly."

"Especially with Jack's help."

"Jack's a great foreman." Uh-oh. She'd said the right words, but with a distracted air that said something else was occupying her mind. "I just worry..." She stopped, looking back at the house.

"About all your little chicks."

"Well, I do. Ever since Lisa came back from New York—"

"She's told you she's fine, and she's asked us to respect that she's an adult."

She *tch*-ed her dismissal of that before adding, "And Dave pretends he's got everything under control. But with Matty gone—"

"Ancient history, Donna. And our plane reservations are going to be in the same category if we don't leave *now*. Besides, you do know they're all waiting at the airport for a sendoff, don't you?"

"Of course. But how do you know?"

"Jack."

She tipped her head. "Jack told you? He says so little—"

He grinned. "He didn't say one word. I saw the note stuck in the visor of his pickup, with the time and date—same as our departure. If we ever get to the airport."

She ignored that last part. "I worry about Jack. He keeps himself so ... separate."

"I know you do, hon, but he's a grown man, and not one of your kids." What Jack Ralston had told him was one of the very few things he hadn't shared with Donna in these past thirty-five years. Jack had asked him not to, and it would have worried her even more than she worried now.

Thirty-five years.

It was hard to believe. Some bad days, but better years than he could have imagined that Christmas night in San Francisco when she said she'd marry him. He'd thought that would be the best day of his life. It had just been the beginning.

Becoming husband and wife. Having Dave, then Lisa. Building the ranch together. Being part of a community. Helping their neighbors. Being helped. Laughing. In a way, she'd taught him how to sing and dance through each day—without his knowing a step or a note.

And now—

"I love the Slash-C," Donna said thickly, as she looked across the land that was their home, that had been the foundation for so much joy.

"I know you do." He cleared his throat, forcing back the lump, making his voice go mock plaintive. "But don't you *want* to go to Paris with me?"

She spun around, stepping into his arms. "Of course I do! Paris and Brittany and Wales and Spain and Ireland and—"

He scooped her up, and set her on the truck seat. "Great. But first we have to get to the airport. And we have to go through Denver, which is always a mess, so if we want to get to Paris..."

"Oh, Denver wasn't so bad to us." Still with tears in her eyes, she smiled as her arms encircled his neck. "I wouldn't mind a few nights on a narrow bed with you in Denver." She kissed him.

He was two-thirds of the way to just crawling in the truck with her right then and calling it a day, when she placed a palm to his cheek and drew back slightly. "But Paris first."

He sucked in a breath. "Right. Paris."

He slammed the truck door on her chuckle, then wasted no time sliding behind the wheel, and getting to the end of the drive, ready to turn onto the highway. There he stopped, though there was no traffic in sight.

He spared a last look at their home in the rearview mirror. She put her hand on his. And then he could look nowhere but at the woman he loved.

"You have changed my life, Donna Roberts Currick." Slowly, he smiled, and named the song no one knew was theirs except for them, " 'They Can't Take That Away From Me.' Any of it. Ever."

"Us," she amended, as one of them always did.

He pulled onto the highway.

"We're on our way, darling."

"We're on our way," she agreed.

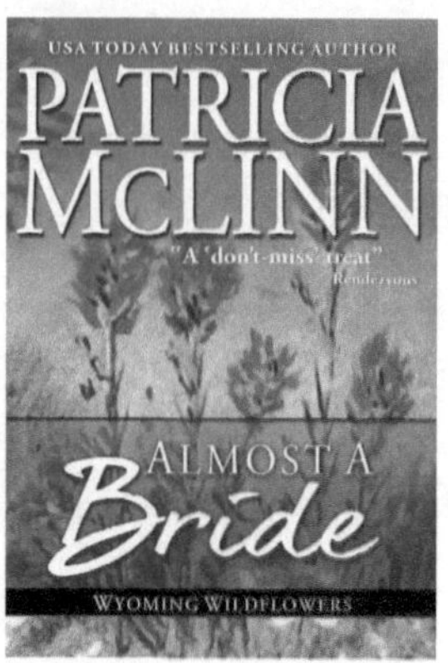

Want more Wyoming Wildflowers? Get Almost a Bride, Book 2 of the Wyoming Wildflower Series!

For news about upcoming Wyoming Wildflowers books, as well as other titles and news, join Patricia McLinn's Readers List and receive her twice-monthly free newsletter.

Enjoy **Wyoming Wildflowers: The Beginning**? (Hope so)

The Curricks' extended family and friends ask if you'll help spread the word about them, the Slash-C ranch and Knighton, Wyoming. You have the power to do that in two quick ways:

Recommend the book and the series to your friends and/or the whole wide world on social media. Shouting from rooftops is particularly appreciated.

Review the book. Take just five minutes to write an honest review and it can make a huge difference. As you likely know, it's the single best way for your fellow readers to find books they'll enjoy, too.

To me—as an author and a reader—the goal is always to find a good author-reader match. By sharing your reading experience through recommendations and reviews, you become a vital matchmaker.

The Wyoming Wildflowers series

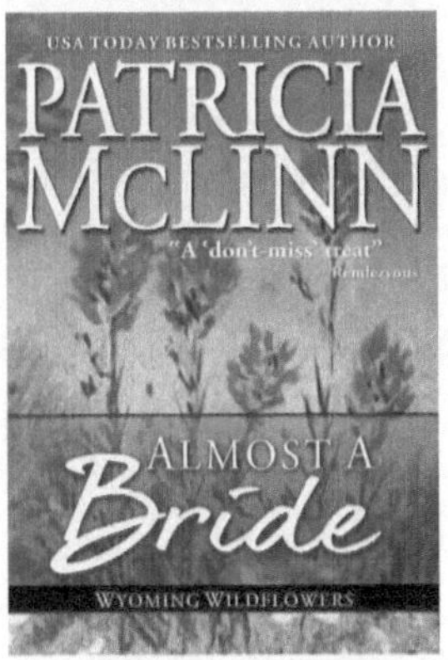

Dave Currick has everything he wants, except the woman he loves…

Almost a Bride

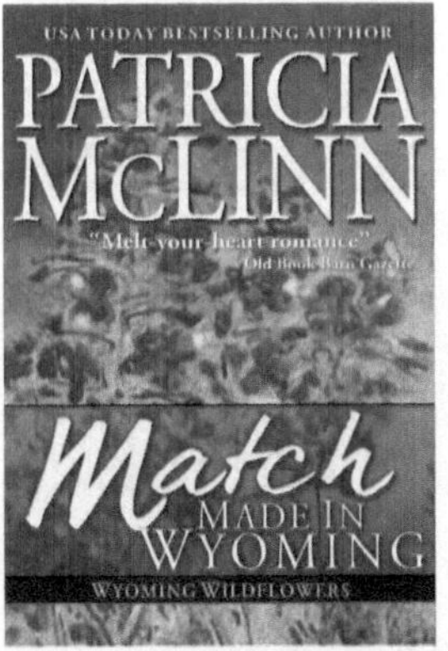

Cal and Taylor can spark a wildfire, but will they come together in…

Match Made in Wyoming

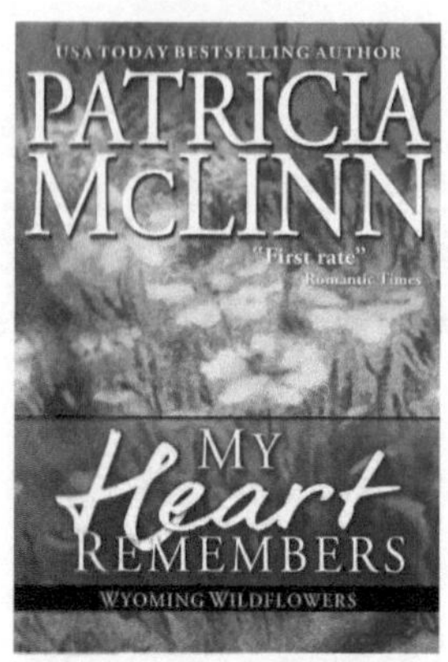

Lisa's carried a secret in her heart for years—and he just hit town…
My Heart Remembers

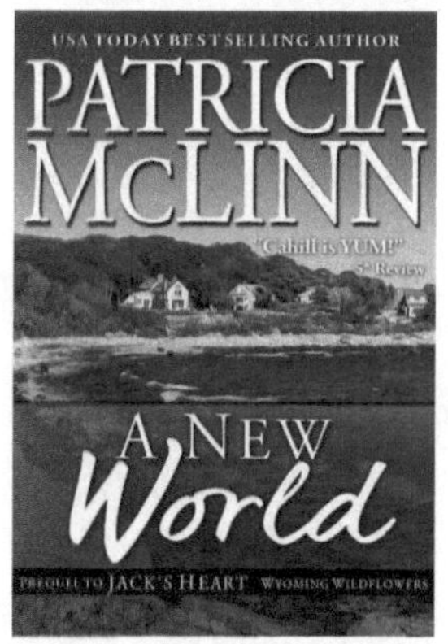

Prequel to Jack's Heart
A New World

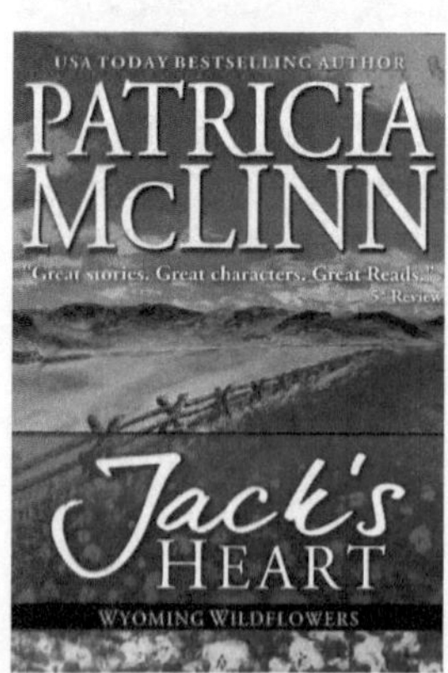

New England single mom meets her Lone Ranger.
Jack's Heart

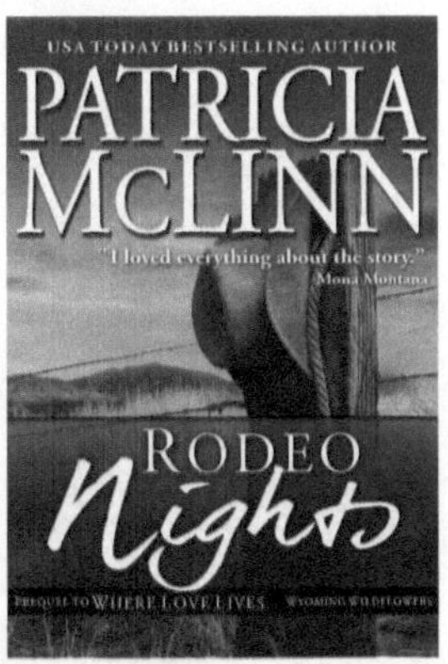

Prequel to Where Love Lives
Rodeo Nights

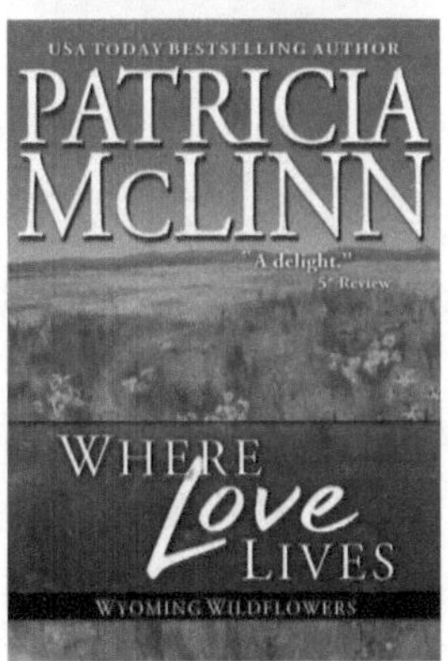

One night stands in the way of Zoe and Matt spending the rest of their days together.
Where Love Lives

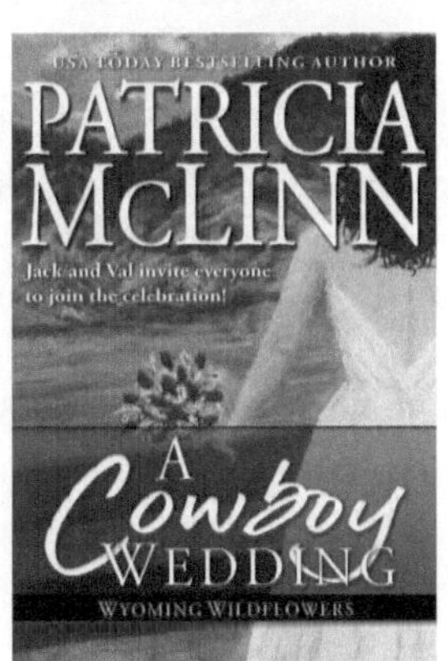

Jack and Val invite you to share the big day with them.

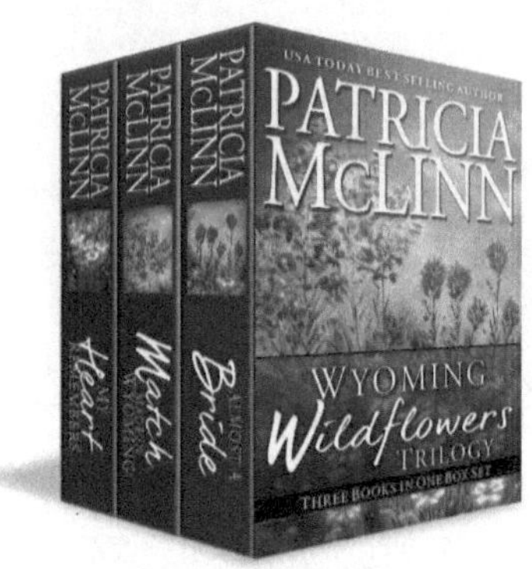

Read three books for one great price in the Wyoming Wildflowers boxed set…

Wyoming Wildflowers Trilogy (Books 2–4)

What people are saying about the WYOMING WILDFLOWERS series

"If you've been feeling burned out and let down by category romance, the Wyoming Wildflowers series will remind you how much there is to love in the genre."

—Writers Club Romance Group on AOL

"While the mystery itself is twisty-turny and thoroughly engaging, it's the smart and witty writing that I loved the best."

—Diane Chamberlain, bestselling author

"I was touched by the love described in this series. Ms. McLinn is the real deal writer. So satisfying."

—Amazon 5* review

If you like western romances, try these other Patricia McLinn series:

The Bardville, Wyoming series

A Place Called Home series

And the stand-alone Ride the River: Rodeo Knights

For more about the contemporary romance series connected to A Cowboy Wedding, check out:

Explore a complete list of all Patricia's books

https://www.patriciamclinn.com/patricias-books

Or get a printable booklist

https://www.patriciamclinn.com/patricias-books/printable-booklist

New! Patricia's eBookstore

(buy digital books online directly from Patricia)

https://www.patriciamclinn.com/patricias-books/ebookstore

More about the Wyoming Wildflowers series

Dear Reader,

This book is the result of requests by readers to discover more about the background of the Currick family. I'm delighted to have shared with you the romance of Donna and Ed Currick. Their love is the foundation for all the Wyoming Wildflowers stories that follow, beginning with their son, Dave, in "Almost a Bride."

To celebrate "Wyoming Wildflowers: The Beginning" I commissioned the lovely painting of snowberry you see on the cover, done in oils by talented Catherine E. Batka.

Look for more stories, more paintings, and more wildflowers, in the future!

Happy reading,

Patricia

About the Author

USA Today bestselling author Patricia McLinn spent more than 20 years as an editor at The Washington Post after stints as a sports writer (Rockford, Ill.) and assistant sports editor (Charlotte, N.C.). She received BA and MSJ degrees from Northwestern University.

McLinn is the author of more than 45 published novels, which are cited by readers and reviewers for wit and vivid characterization. Her books include mysteries, romantic suspense, contemporary romance, historical romance and women's fiction. They have topped bestseller lists and won numerous regional and national awards.

She has spoken about writing from Melbourne, Australia, to Washington, D.C., including being a guest-speaker at the Smithsonian Institution.

McLinn, who lives in Northern Kentucky, loves to hear from readers through her website, Facebook and Twitter.

Visit with Patricia:

Website: https://www.patriciamclinn.com

Facebook: facebook.com/PatriciaMcLinn

Twitter: @PatriciaMcLinn

Pinterest: pinterest.com/patriciamclinn

ALMOST A BRIDE

Wyoming Wildflowers
Book 2

Patricia McLinn

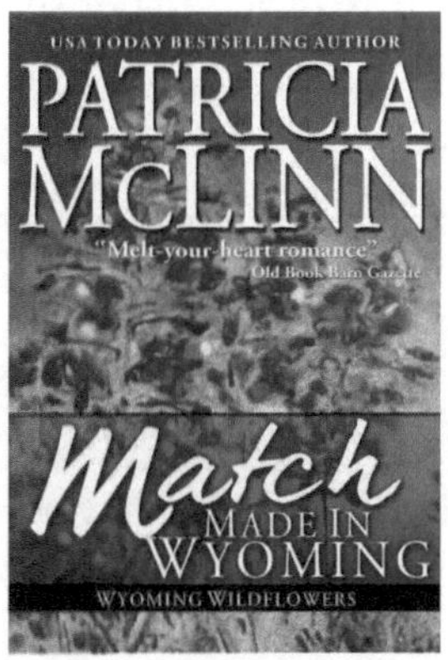

Matty Brennan has thought of one last, long shot to save her family's Wyoming ranch when she runs into the one man who might could make the long shot work—the same man who broke her heart six years ago....

"This is business," she informed Dave Currick with every scrap of dignity she could muster. "Sort of a ... a business proposition."

"Well, I'd be happy to talk to you about business, but I'm heading for an appointment right now.

"It's just that my business is important," she said stiffly. "Very important."

"I could come see you tomorrow—"

"No!" Twenty-four hours? No way. If she thought about this too much—if she thought about it at *all*—she'd lose her nerve. Or regain her pride. "It's, well, it's real important to me. It's urgent."

"Urgent?" Now he was frowning. "Are you okay, Matty? Is something wrong?"

"No. I mean, yes, but not the way you mean."

She took a deep breath and looked around. A young couple was coming up the steps at one end of the sidewalk, probably heading toward the real estate office next to Taylor's. Matty grabbed the rolled back cuff of Dave's white shirt and tugged him toward the opposite end, where they'd have more privacy.

"What is it, Matty? You're worrying me. Is it that Cal Ruskoff you've got working for you?"

She stared up into his narrowed hazel eyes in astonishment. "Cal? No. Why would you think that? He's great. Works like five men and never complains."

Dave's frown didn't ease, but some of the tension went out of his broad shoulders. "Then what is it?"

"Give me a second here," she said irritably.

She tried to think of a way to say this, a way to make it more palatable, and couldn't. It was like going into the swimming hole on a spring day when they were kids. There was no edging into it, inch by inch, or you'd never do it. The only way to go was to take the plunge.

She took a breath and leaped.

"I want to marry you."

For a second, she could almost believe she'd really jumped into the swimming hole. She felt the same shock of cold surround her and the same sensation that all sound in the world was muffled and distant. The only thing she could hear clearly was the beating of her own heart.

Then a single word from Dave brought her back.

"Pardon?"

He hadn't moved an inch and his expression hadn't changed. He sounded as if he was certain—as only Dave could be certain—that he'd heard wrong.

Of course he was going to make her repeat it. Dave had never made anything easy on her. Not since he'd told her, then all of five years old, that if she couldn't keep up, she should go back and play with dolls.

"I want to marry you. In fact, I *have* to marry you."

He seemed to come out of a trance. He pushed his cowboy hat back off his forehead, and leaned against the pole that held up the roof over the sidewalk, crossing one leg over the other with an air of total nonchalance.

"Have to? You sure it's me you're thinking of?" The amusement was back in his voice. At least she thought it was amusement. It had an edge to it and the look he was giving her didn't strike her as a laughing matter, but maybe that's how he showed amusement these days. After all, she hadn't been around him for years. "Darlin', either I missed something in the past few weeks that I'd truly hate to think I'd missed or you're setting to make medical history. Unless there's someone else more, let's say, recent?"

"Don't be an idiot, Dave. I'm not pregnant."

"That's a relief. I'd hate to have you be the subject of all those tabloid newspapers for bearing a child six years after the fact. As for the more usual time frame, well a gentleman doesn't like to think he's forgotten things like that. And if someone else—"

"Oh, shut up, Dave. It's nothing like that."

"Nothing to do with oh, say, an affair of the heart?"

"Why would it have to do with an affair of the heart?"

"Well," he drawled, "marriage sometimes does."

"Not this time. I told you, it's business."

"Business?" he asked politely. "I'm sorry. I'm not following this. Call me stupid, but I associate marriage with romance, not business."

"Yeah, right. You've had enough romances to make Don Juan look like Barney Fife, and I've never heard anything about you getting married."

"Been paying attention to my social life, have you?"

"It's like the wind around here—it's only remarkable when it's not making its presence felt."

"Matty, if this is the way you ask all the men to marry you, I can see why you're still single. I thought I taught you better than that."

"*You* taught—Why you…"

She swallowed the words with the greatest of effort. He'd gotten under her skin from their earliest days. Even when she'd thought she was in love with him, he'd been able to yank her chain with the flick of his finger. But no more. And certainly not now. She couldn't afford it. The Flying W couldn't afford it.

"This is all beside the point." She barely gritted her teeth at all; she was proud of that.

"And what is the point, Matty?" His mouth twitched.

"The point—" She figured she couldn't be blamed for a little teeth-gritting now. "—is that I want us to get married. Right away. But only temporarily."

"Temporarily?"

"Of course, temporarily." She was miffed. "You don't think I'd ask you to get married for good, do you?"

"I didn't mean any disrespect. But not having been proposed to before, at least not by you—" She glared at him. Because of the mock humble tone; not, definitely not, because of his intimation that he might have been proposed to by other women. "—I want to keep this all straight. Orderly. Since it's business. Isn't that what you said?"

"That's what I said. We'd get married, then after a while, we'd get divorced. Uncontested. Nice and clean."

He raised one eyebrow. "Not sure I've ever heard of a clean divorce, much less a nice one."

"That's because all those other divorces were between people who were married."

"You got me there, Matty, That's a fact."

"Oh, quit with the Gary Cooper act, Currick. You know what I mean. We would be *pretending* to be married. I mean, we'd *get* married, but we wouldn't *be* married. We wouldn't—" She shot him a glowering look to be sure he got her point. "—do *things* married couples do. So the divorce would be no big deal."

He rubbed his chin. God, he'd gone from Gary Cooper to Gabby Hayes. If he said *Well, Goooolllleeee*, she'd belt him.

"Uh-huh. Okay, so we get married—without really *being* married—and then we get divorced. I have that right?"

"Yes."

"How long?"

"How long what?"

"Before we get divorced?"

She hadn't thought that out yet. If the Flying W didn't get the grant this year or if one year's grant wasn't enough to get it back on its feet, she'd be back where she'd started. Better give herself some leeway.

"Five years."

He jerked up from the pole as if it had caught fire. "Five years!"

She crossed her arms and braced her legs. "Five years isn't a life sentence, you know. It's not like we'd have to be together all the time. We'd only have to make it look like we were married."

He rested back against the pole. "So it would be okay if I fooled around on the side?"

"No!" She would have taken that back if she could, especially when he got smug. "We have to keep up proper appearances. That's part of the deal."

"Matty, honey, be reasonable. Unless you're going to rethink your position on conjugal rights—"

"No!"

"—And you don't want me running around on you, five years is definitely out of the question."

She gave in with ill grace. "Four years, then."

"Six months."

"No way. Three years."

"One year."

"Two years."

"Eighteen months."

She figured furiously in her head. She'd just *have* to get the grant this year. Surely she could turn the Flying W around with two years' worth of grants. And paperwork for a divorce would take time, so with some luck ... "Twenty-two months before we start the divorce proceedings."

"Done."

He stuck out his hand. She put hers in it. He wrapped his big hand around hers, the calluses slightly abrading the tender skin across the back of her hand and the strength of his fingers pressing against hers. You'd think a lawyer would have soft skin and strength only in the muscles used for endorsing checks.

"So twenty-two months from now we get divorced. When do we get married?"

Still holding her hand, he leaned back against the pole, unbalancing her enough that she had to take a step toward him to keep from falling over. She yanked her hand free.

"As fast as we can." The application deadline for this year's grant was in three and a half weeks.

For a long moment, he stared at her from the shadow cast by his hat—able to see out so much better than she could see in. "Okay," he said at last.

Matty let out a breath—and an instant later realized she'd relaxed too soon.

"Now, what do I get out of this deal?"

JACK'S HEART

Wyoming Wildflowers
Book 5

Patricia McLinn

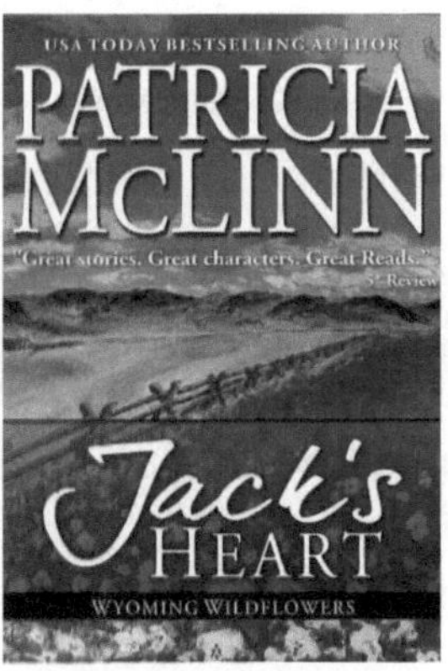

It hadn't been her best decision.

And that was saying something, considering the not-great decisions she'd made in her life.

Including getting pregnant by a guy she now recognized she'd known in her bones wasn't the guy for her.

Including heading as far away as possible from her family in Gloucester, Massachusetts.

Every last one of them would have rallied around her. Which was precisely why she'd gone to Port Orchard, Washington.

She'd gotten into this on her own, she needed to handle it on her own.

Valerie Trimarco, woman in charge.

Right.

Although, she had done okay in Port Orchard these past months. She'd supported herself, made some good friends, had everything arranged for the birth.

Everything lined up and ready to go.

Right up until this overwhelming need to have the baby in Gloucester—to be *home*—swamped every island of sense she possessed. All thoughts of handling things on her own or even with the help of her friends disappeared. All she could think of was getting home.

So she'd packed her car and headed for Massachusetts.

That still wasn't such an awful decision. After all, they said it wasn't a great idea to fly this close to the due date. She liked driving alone. And her car was reliable and sturdy.

Though even reliable and sturdy cars eventually run out of gas if they're kept running.

But keeping it running for brief periods for spurts of warmth had seemed like the reasonable thing to do once the car got stuck.

Of course it wouldn't have gotten stuck if she hadn't had to swerve to avoid that cow when she came around the curve in the road.

On the other hand, she wouldn't have been on this road if she hadn't had to keep changing her route because of the storm sweeping down from the northwest. From the last report she'd heard, I-94 should be closed right about now.

So she'd made the right decision to take 1-90 out of Billings, even though it had soon become clear the storm would hit her before she could get far enough east to get ahead of it.

She'd adjusted again, planning to reach Buffalo, then swing south by way of I-25 to connect with I-80, which also ran east-west, but— she hoped—far enough south to miss the storm.

That was not to be, either.

She'd caught a radio report that said there was a backup before

Buffalo from an accident that had spread gravel across the highway. By the time it could be cleaned up, the storm would be on top of them and no one would be going anywhere.

So she'd gotten off the interstate, creating her own detour. She'd taken a road south. When it ran out, she turned east. That road gave up, too, so she picked up another heading south. And did another east-south combo before she reached this one. She'd been heading east quite a while, so she really should have reached the Interstate … if it hadn't been for that cow.

The cow and the ditch.

Pushing had been out of the question, considering her condition, but she'd tried rocking the car out of the ditch like the trained-to-drive in snow New Englander she was. Alas, no amount of rocking helped when the nose of your station wagon was sucking in mud from the far side of the ditch.

And then the wind picked up, blowing around curtains of snow. Not light and airy sheers, either. More like heavy velvet.

This was not good.

A sound and a shadow—later, she never could remember which caught her attention first—jerked her head to look out the window of the driver's door.

It looked like a brown blanket was hanging nearly next to the window with—was that a boot?

Another sound came, this one like a voice, though she couldn't make out words.

Then, at the very top of the field of vision allowed by the window, she saw a pair of eyes. She blinked, then squinted, finally making sense of what she was seeing.

It was a man on a horseback. He'd bent nearly double, apparently to look into the window. He had a scarf muffling the lower part of his face, and a cowboy hat held on with another scarf covering the top part, leaving only the eyes.

"Ma'am? You okay?" He shouted it this time, and she realized it was what he'd said before.

She pressed the window button to lower the window a few inches. At least there was enough juice left for that. She hoped there'd be enough to raise it again, because it was going to get very cold in the car very fast with the window even partially open.

"Where am I?"

"Ma'am?"

"Don't look at me like I've lost my marbles." Though that was mostly an assumption, since all she had to judge by were his eyes. "I know I'm somewhere in Wyoming, and I should be real close to I-25."

He'd tugged his hat even lower after her first words. "You're on the Slash-C Ranch, and you're about six miles from the Interstate."

"Hah! I knew I was getting close."

"But you've been running parallel to it for however long you've been on this road."

"Damn." She must have gotten her souths and easts confused at some point. A mini-contraction playfully stabbed her. "Damn, damn, *DAMN!*"

She panted as the contraction ebbed, knowing it wasn't anywhere near to the worst, since she'd already had a few of those.

"Ma'am, are you okay?" he asked again.

"Depends on what you mean by okay."

She had the impression of a frown from under the brim of the cowboy hat. "Pardon?"

"If you mean do I have any broken bones or other injuries, no. If you mean am I as well off as the cow I swerved to miss that ambled off looking for more grass to eat, no again. I admit this wasn't my best decision, coming off the Interstate to try to beat the weather, but it really shouldn't have turned out this bad."

"You're not hurt and your vehicle still runs—"

"I'm not hurt, but I am in pain. And my vehicle as you call it won't run long because it's about out of gas."

"I'll ride back and get you some gas—"

"You missed the part about me being in pain. I—"

She broke off, because this contraction was not a mini and it wasn't playful. She concentrated on trying to remember her training, trying not to tense up, trying to keep the hiss through her teeth a hiss and not a scream.

"Ma'am? *Ma'am?*"

Now she'd done it. She'd rattled the cowboy.

The contraction eased, not quite passing, however.

"I'm in labor," she said with uncharacteristic brevity.

His head ducked lower, apparently for a better look into the car window. "Shit."

"That about covers it. And I'm no expert, but I think this kid's eager to see the world. Just like her mother. So that's probably a good sign that we'll get along, and this motherhood thing should—"

She quit because the cowboy was leaving. Without even getting off his horse. He'd just turned the horse and started back along the side of her wagon toward the road. She stuck her head out the window and saw the swish of horse's tail as it stepped up the embankment toward the road.

She couldn't believe it.

But she could. Because it was exactly the kind of outcome that resulted from most of her decisions. Still, you'd think the guy would have at least said something—

A sound from the passenger side of the car yanked her head around to it.

Over the top of the shade to her favorite lamp that had survived the slide into the ditch because the passenger seat was packed as tightly as the rest of the car, she realized there was something outside that frosted window.

Two somethings. The cowboy and horse shape had separated into two separate shapes. The cowboy shape was looping the reins around the passenger door handle.

He hadn't left her.

Her eyes felt hot, but tears didn't form.

He hadn't left *them*.

Then he shouted something through the closed window she

couldn't possibly make out. She closed her window before opening the passenger window, because she wasn't a complete idiot, and if there was only enough juice for one move she wanted it to be to *close* a window. This way if it stopped working after she opened the passenger window there'd only be one window letting a blizzard in.

He shouted again.

"Wait a second," she snapped. Then the window was down.

"I said release the tailgate. And—"

"Why?"

"—Put this window back up so it doesn't let more cold in."

"I know. Why do you think—?"

But the cowboy shape was moving, leaving the horse shape by the passenger door.

She raised the window, but that didn't help much because in another moment, he had the tailgate open.

"What are you—?"

"Quiet," he ordered. "Working."

"Like you can't talk and work at the same ti—"

Another contraction cut her off. This one was different. She couldn't say it hurt more, because they all hurt. But it seemed more *serious*. She wanted to pull her knees up, but the steering wheel prevented it. She concentrated on breathing. *Focus. Focus. Focus...*

What was that sound?

As the contraction relented, she recognized she'd been hearing the sound for a while.

The cowboy was moving her things around on the deck of the old station wagon.

"Hey, what are you doing?"

He didn't respond.

She started to turn to see what he was doing, thought better of it, and tilted the rear view mirror.

She could only see to the back in part of the mirror's view. In the rest, he'd piled her belongings up to the roof, doing the same on the sides, apparently.

"I won't be able to drive," she protested. "You're blocking all my sight lines." She prided herself on her driving. Even family who gave her grief for being impulsive, restless, and having wanderlust acknowledged she was a great driver. A little fast, maybe, but safe.

In the mirror, she saw a portion of his cowboy hat come up, as if he might be looking toward her. "You're not driving anywhere anytime soon."

"Couldn't you get a tow truck?"

"I've radioed the home ranch. They're coming."

"Good. That's good. Then we can just wait." She didn't feel one bit guilty for roping him into that *we* waiting. Besides, it was better than riding around in a snowstorm. Except … "I don't know where you'll sit, though."

"Making room back here."

"You're going to sit back there?" That didn't seem very sociable.

"Both of us."

At the moment, with the cold streaming in from the open tailgate, the prospect of being near some body heat had appeal. "Will there be room?"

"Yeah." He sounded grim. "Got any more blankets?"

"There's a box—"

"Got that. Need more for—this will do."

She saw a flash of scarlet in the mirror, tried to twist around again, found that wasn't a good idea again. "Hey, what was that I just saw? Was that my cape?"

"Dunno."

"Long, hooded, cashmere, lined with satin, my favorite piece of clothing ever."

He wasn't listening. Because partway through her description, he'd backed out of the tailgate and dropped it closed behind him.

How hard was it to recognize a cape? Didn't take a fashion expert for heaven's sake, so—

Her door opened abruptly.

"What were you doing with my cape?" she demanded. No sense

wasting time confirming it was her cape when she couldn't think of anything else she had that was that color.

"Put your arms around my neck."

"What?"

"Put your arms around my neck."

"I heard you," she said a little testily, but she figured she was entitled. "Let's try *why*?"

"So I can carry you to the back."

"Carry me? *Carry* me? Do you have any idea how heavy I am?"

"Less than a bale of hay."

That stopped her, because she had no idea how much a bale of hay weighed. And while she was stopped, he scooped her up.

Out of self-preservation she put her arms around his neck. She figured if he started to drop her she could hold onto his neck long enough to soften her landing.

"And you're having to carry me through snow," she added.

"Been in snow before."

His breath puffed warm across the slice of her chin exposed between her pulled-down knit cap and the scarf wrapped up around her chin and mouth.

"Why are you doing this? I was fine where I was." Sort of.

"More room."

The wind had strengthened. If his mouth hadn't been practically in her ear she might not have heard his low voice through all the layers of cloth.

"Doesn't take that much room to wait. You said somebody's coming from this ranch of yours so——"

"Not mine. I'm foreman. Not owner."

"Ownership is not real important to me at the moment."

He grunted. Might have been part of a chuckle. Might have been in pain from trying to support her elephant-like body.

He turned the corner to the back of the car, and the going got a bit easier, apparently because he'd tamped down the snow during his box-rearranging. He set her on her feet, and lifted the tailgate.

He'd created a sort of elliptical nest in the middle, cushioning the deck with blankets and—

"My cape!" She snatched the nearest section of fabric and reeled it in, bundling the fabric in her arms.

He moved as if he intended to lift her again. She evaded it by swinging her arm away, and nearly lost her balance on the snowpack underfoot. She saved herself by sitting—hard—on the edge of the tailgate.

"Can you get in by yourself?" he asked doubtfully.

"Yes."

And she did. By inching herself backward like a panting, heaving cross between a crab and a rhinoceros. Each time she moved backward she scrunched up the blankets a bit, and he pulled them down.

As soon as she got far enough in that—with her knees bent—the tailgate could be closed without performing a double footectomy on her she flopped back, trying to replenish her oxygen. The wadded up fabric of the cape sat on her chest. She watched it rise and fall with each breath.

She supposed she should be grateful she hadn't had another contraction during these maneuvers.

"Okay?"

Her eyes flicked to him. He'd come up beside her without her even noticing his movement. In other words, he climbed in like it was the easiest thing in the world. Damn him. "You're kidding, right?"

He made that sound again, and since he was no longer carrying her, she had to conclude it had more to do with amusement than pain.

"I'm gonna radio again."

In the time she took two breaths, he was out and had dropped the tailgate down, cutting off the wind.

She started trying to fold the cape, so she could put it somewhere safe. But the voluminous flow of fabric made it more than a little tricky while she was lying down and with barely enough room to stretch her arms up to their full length.

She could just make out his voice over the wind, which probably meant he was shouting into the radio. She listened harder, trying to assess his tone.

Neutral. Matter-of-fact. That was the best she could do.

Then she felt the serious pain edging back in. Sliding in inexorably, like an oilslick being brought to shore by the tide.

She fisted her hands in the cape's material, the concept of folding jettisoned.

Each swell, rising a little higher, carrying the black, foul-smelling blob of pain a little closer until—

"How're you doing?" he said from someplace close by. He had to be, right? She couldn't hear him that clearly if he were outside, but she hadn't heard him get in—Oh, hell, who cared?

"The contractions are coming—Oh … Oh, God!" Pain swallowed the universe and her along with it. There was nothing but pain. There would never be anything but pain.

It receded, but she knew that was just a ploy so it could hurt more the next time. Higher and closer with every swell. She knew the ocean's ways. This was an ocean of pain.

But at least, for now, it let her see what was around her. She looked up into the cowboy's face.

He was partially kneeling beside her, his hat was gone. He had light brown hair with a weird dent in it. And eyes somewhere between blue and gray.

"My cousin has gray eyes," she said between pants. Why was she panting like she'd just run ten miles?

He frowned. "That so?"

"That's so. Eleanor Thatcher—McRae. Can't forget the McRae becau—"

She screamed. Not like at a scary part in a movie scream, where you follow up with a nervous laugh. But a scream like when the pain that swallowed you had all its knives out slicing every little bit of you.

When she reached the border between the ocean of pain where she would never leave and the world that other people inhabited, she realized the cowboy had his hand on her forehead, stroking back her hair.

"You're going to have that baby soon."

"Can't. Water hasn't—" She panted the words out. She didn't have her breath back from the pain or the scream or both. "—broken."

"Doesn't always happen until after. We're going to deliver it here."

"Here? Don't be silly. We can't—"

"We can."

He said it so simply, she began to believe. "Have you delivered a baby before?"

"Yes."

She looked up into his eyes. They were very calm. Yet, sad. So sad. Why would he be so sad? Because she was going to die? But he'd just said he'd delivered babies before, so … "Oh, shit, you mean *cows?*"

"Cows and horses and sheep and dogs."

She gestured to herself. "Human!" Then at her abdomen, "Human baby!"

"It's all nature."

"I don't think so. I'm not—"

"You're going to have this baby. Here. And soon. And nobody else is going to get here before you do. It's you and me."

She locked eyes with him and opened her mouth to point out again what a stupid, horrible, bad, bad, *bad* idea this was. His calm, sad eyes stared back at her.

She said, "You and me."

"Right. I'm going to need some room. So—" He hooked her under her arms and slid her more toward the front of the car. She was sitting up more than she had been, which was slightly more comfortable. Like being on a bed of pins instead of needles.

He spread the cape over her, then started backing up.

"Where are you going?" She didn't sound panicked, because she didn't panic. She was up for anything. Ready for any adventure. Yes, sir. That was her.

"We gotta get you out of these pants. Fast." He opened the tailgate and stepped out, having to remain bent over so he didn't hit his head.

He started on her shoes, but left her socks on.

"Won't be hard. I haven't worn anything but elastic for months. Never thought I'd miss zippers, but—Wait. Wait!" He'd started to tug on the bottom of the pant legs, which were cooperating like they thought they were going to get some action.

"Contraction?"

"No." The pants were gone. He draped the side of the cape over her, moving more things around. Making room for where he'd have to be when she—"This is going to happen. This is really going to happen. Here. Now."

"Yes."

"And you're going to use my cape."

"Yes."

She loved that cape. This kid better be worth it. And if anyone else ever said anything like that about her precious baby she would scoop their heart out with her fingernails. "Oh, God, at least tell me your name."

"Jack, Ma'am. Jack Ralston."

"I'm Valerie. Valerie Trimarco. Or Val. Lots of people call me Val."

"Ma'am." He crawled back in beside her, tugging the tailgate closed after him. The wind howled at having its fun thwarted.

"If you call me Ma'am one more time, I swear I will not try to muffle my screams one little bit."

His mouth quirked. "Okay, Valerie."

"Okay. As long as we understand each other." For no reason other than the reasons that had been staring her in the face for hours, some of them for months, her eyes welled with tears. And then the well ran over. "Oh, God, Jack Ralston, what are we going to do?"

He leaned over her, looking her straight in the eyes. "We're going to have this baby, Ma—Val. You and me."

"You and me," she repeated.

"And everything's going to be okay."

www.ingramcontent.com/pod-product-compliance
Lightning Source LLC
Chambersburg PA
CBHW031248210726
48287CB00003B/942